CRIES FOR HELP, VARIOUS

CRIES FOR HELP, VARIOUS

STORIES

PADGETT POWELL

CATAPULT NEW YORK

Published by Catapult
catapult.co

ISBN: 978-1-936787-31-9

Some of these stories, some in different form, were previously
published in *The Cincinnati Review, Columbia: A Journal of
Literature and Art, Cutbank, Epoch, FENCE, Gulf Coast, The
Hopkins Review, The Idaho Review, Iron Horse Literary Review,
The Land-Grant College Review, Little Star, McSweeney's,
NarrativeMagazine.com, New England Review, Okey-Panky, Oxford
American, The Paris Review, St. Petersburg Review, Subtropics,
Unsaid*, and *The Washington Post Magazine*.

"The Imperative Mood" was first published as an ebook by Profile
Books in the United Kingdom. "Working for Brother Catcard"
and "Utopia" were published in an ebook by Ecco Press.

"Joplin and Dickens" contains quotations from Charles Dickens's
Oliver Twist and *Bleak House*.

Catapult titles are distributed to the trade by
Publishers Group West
Phone: 800-788-3123

Library of Congress Control Number 2015933695

Designed by Strick&Williams

Printed in Canada

9 8 7 6 5 4 3 2 1

For Uncle Don and Spode, my teachers

Contents

Horses

The other horse traders are over there in the 7-Eleven. These horses are jittery and I don't know how long I can hold them. That piebald one there—or is that a paint? It's a Holstein for all I know, and that is one of the galling things about this enterprise, people saying the roan this and the buckskin and the paint and the quarter and the Indian pony and that and this and you have no idea which goddamn horse they are talking about, they are talking about one of fifty things we have here which can get us hung if we are caught, can kill you if you get near one in the wrong way, and can run off and get you beat to shit by the hombres who affect to know how not to have them run away, I have just about had it with this shit, what with most of the crew over there in the 7-Eleven and the Sheriff cruising around out here, around me and the herd and the hot dog wrappers, and the horses are nervous in the wind and the swinging stoplights, and all the fellows with the handlebar mustaches are inside getting coffee, and I'm out here looking like a plebe in a fraternity with fifty stolen monsters I can't tell apart, and there's the Sheriff, and we are beyond the day when he can be shot and we go on our way.

Do not ask me how I am involved in rustling horses in the 21st century over asphalt with the law in big Ford Crown Victorias. I do not know. They are in there in goddamn period chaps and I am out here in Army Navy discount camo fatigues I got for five dollars. I look like a dope dealer. I'd feel better if I were a dope dealer. You will not believe what we are up to. No one will credit what we are up to. I do not myself. If the Sheriff interrogated me right now about these fifty horses by the highway with their drovers in the 7-Eleven getting coffee, and I told him the whole story, he would not believe what we are up to.

The silhouette of a man—rather like the Tin Man, they said, improbable large straight lines and a hollow sound from it—stood in the doorway during what must have been a big cowboy drunk, or a big cowboy-poetry drunk, because I am convinced also that some of these drovers are cowboy poets, given their proclivity to be on the phone and their attention to their costumes and their pallid postures and the way they seem to want to hear themselves talk and what can start a fistfight (one said another used too many feminine endings and the second asked just what was that supposed to mean and hit him) . . . where was I? I have a headache, it is snowing lightly, the 7-Eleven still holds twenty poet horse rustlers, I am telling you what you cannot believe: that a Tin Man came to these men in their revelries preceding the current larcenous overland march and told them, in a thundery but soft voice, to take horses into the Big Horn and to be ambushed by an equal or larger band of Indians and surrender them, the horses, to the Indians, and by so doing initiate a reversal of history that would at the other end of its drift restore thirty million buffalo to the Plains and his integrity and livelihood and independent character to the red man. "Reverse history?" one of the cowboys is reputed to have said. "We gave them the horse in the first place. To reverse history we'd have to take the horses away, it seems to—"

"Sewerage," the Tin Man said, or some aural approximation thereto, for the sound from the thing was soft and not trippingly tongued, which lent a force to its supernatural-seeming authority. A foul odor, identical to sewerage, then filled the barracks, as they like to call their quarters, and some of the more excitable ones maintain that a soup of actual septic-tank flotsam then filled the room to a level of two feet before receding cleanly away, but other witnesses, the more formal of the poets, in my estimate, ascribe this vision to the overactive imaginations of their lesser trained and less reliable brothers. Nonetheless they all obeyed the call of the vision, stole fifty horses, and now drink patriotically large quantities of gourmet-blend coffee from convenience stores en route to reversing history and righting the colossal imperialist genocide of the West, while I hold the horses. The horses are the starter culture, as I see it, if this history we are to reverse could be viewed as yogurt, and I don't see that that is an inapt conceit. That is my exact plan if I find myself interviewed alone by the Sheriff, in fact: I will tell him the horses are starter culture, and that is all I will say other than asking they appoint me a lawyer, and a psychiatrist if that comes with the deal now. Hanging out with men wearing Polo clothes and affecting to punch each other over the matter of feminine endings should alone establish a sound insanity plea. I will walk away from the horse-stealing charge.

"Boy, what you doin' with all that horseflesh?" the Sheriff finally asks, purring loudly beside me and the herd in his big throaty Ford.
"I have succumbed to deer pressure," I tell him. At this he smiles.

3

"Y'all need a permit drive livestock loose up a road like iss."

"Sir, what is that?" I indicate a jar of dark-colored liquid on the seat beside him.

"That? Blackstrap molasses. Boy give it to me dudn' want me lookin in t'is business."

"Could I have a taste?"

"You can have the whole thang, son. I'mone bust that boy for whatever it is he doin' pretty soon."

I have had a fascination with sorghum and molasses for some time because I do not know what they are. I finger up a taste of the stuff and pour a quantity of it into the ankle collars of each of my boots and step about a bit to get the molasses into the socks and crackling good. The Sheriff smiles at this too. This will keep me out of the Big Horn culture-reversing ambush.

"Sheriff, I need to go to the hospital."

"I see that, boy."

"Could you take me?"

"I can call you a amblance but I can't take you myself, it's regulations—"

"Aw for*get* it, Sheriff. I'll walk." I affect to start for the hospital, abandoning the horses. I wonder if the poets will appreciate my forestalling and deflecting the Arm of the Law from their date with the Indians. The Sheriff lurches the big car up to me and pops it in park before it has stopped and chirps to a passionate little stop beside me in the huge idling machine. Now he is not smiling.

"I feel the same way. About all this"—he feels at something on his face and looks at himself in his side mirror—"regulations shit. Get in the car. You need help."

I get in, rider-side front. The Sheriff says, "What did you do that for?" as I with some difficulty gum and crackle my feet into the car.

"Do what?"

"Nothin'."

We ride, and we ride well, and I never see the horses or the poets again. I do not read of a reversal of history that begins at the Big Horn. They did not admit me to the hospital but told me to get my nasty shoes back outside.

An orderly seeing me taffy out, by this time hobbling as if I am in ankle chains, ripping blisters and wincing, caught up to me outside the ER and provided me with a small handle to a spigot and I washed my boots in cold water from the side of the hospital and then returned the spigot handle to him.

"Old guy in here last night?" he said.

"Yeah?"

"Come in here moaning and shit, like food poison?"

"Yeah?"

"He get all booked in? They put him in a room? The doctor gerng come?"

"Yeah?"

"Well, that dude *exploded*!"

"What?"

"Shit all over the room. Had to get his ass brand-new room. I been cleaning it since five this mornin'. That why I have this handle."

We look at my wet boots and socks on the grass, exhausted. As mornings go, or days, this one has been, for me, singularly good. I feel ennobled to have distracted the Sheriff, abandoned my role in reversing history, and now to be a boon companion to a man who has mopped shit in a room since five a.m. We are the ungainfully employed, unjailed, unlettered, unprotected fair boys left in the world. I feel a little high with my numb feet on the green grass beside my sodden socks and boots, my new friend smiling at them and not asking one question about them, or me, or the Sheriff, whom he saw deposit me in the ER drive-thru. These are lousy details of the quotidian and they do not merit the attention of men thinking about larger things, like cleaning whole rooms fouled by unfortunate exploding men.

"He had six hundred dollar in his wallet, in his pants, hook on the wall, all spray with shit. I took ten dollar. Only. I put his clothes in the laundry. Special service. Ten-dollar tip, moreso."

"I dig where you comin' from."

"Dude *esploded*."

The way this fellow shakes his head, incredulously admiring the misfortune of the exploding patient, and the way we snicker together on the lawn, is pleasing, very pleasing, in the long array of not final things during our time on Earth. The way the day has gone has made me think things like "the not final things during our time on Earth." I am happy, happy not to be a horse-rustling poet, a culture starter, on a lawn with cold blue feet in the sun, my bowels not urgent, a friend to chat with.

Love

I walk around picking up raw bits of meat in the soles of my shoes. The old Converse high-tops pick up the meat and apparently mold it into these rather blunted pyramid-shaped nougats, or pills, what would you call compacted meat in roughly the shape of pyramids such as what fall out, a little dusty, from your shoes? I have these Docksiders with a wavy razor-cut tread that picks the meat up into the thin voids of the tread and presses it into ribbons that suggest tapeworms, or would suggest tapeworms were you to get the meat out of the tread in a piece. Meat pressed into shapes like that is disturbing to me somehow, so I am not unhappy that it can't be got out in that configuration, the tapeworm or audio-mylar configuration, but I am not altogether happy that it, the meat, remains up in the razory tread of my shoes either. I *wash* the shoes but am not convinced you can really *clean* up in spaces that tight. I question the design, the intellect that decided to cut rubber into waved micrometer slices to shoe men who want to be sailors at heart, or even pretend sailors on sidewalks in their chinos hailing their girls, etc. The waffle-iron idea of the Converse engineers seems by comparison a much more wholesome approach. I am going with the flow mostly here. I am mostly going with the flow here, I mean. Trying to, with meat on my shoes. I know a poet named Rachel.

September is my yellow month. I can be down in the mouth but not blue in my yellow month. Rachel is pink. I am not going to mention her again, at the request of one of my friends.

Joplin and Dickens

Janis Joplin at her desk regards Charlie Dickens at his, and wonders. That boy could be the answer, or one of the answers, to the long question that will trouble her. Will I be the loneliest girl on Earth? The dog of loneliness is already at age nine nuzzling her. Because it is, after all, a dog, and nuzzling, and she nine, the dog of loneliness nuzzling little Janis Joplin at this point is merely cute. It will not be so cute later when she has bad skin and has wrecked her voice and swings that bottle of Southern Comfort at it as it tries to lick her face all sweaty on stages . . . oh my this is poetic. Let's abjure poetry because the conceit of this—Janis Joplin and Mr. Dickens a century out of his time—is already inane. We will stick to the facts and try not to be pretty.

She has heard Charlie Dickens use pretty big words early in the third grade. Unlike other children she has not been inclined to roll her eyes at him when he deploys a doozy. Even the teacher has rolled her eyes, or done that thing where she takes a deep breath and lets it out and says, "Okay, Charlie, can you state that in other words?"

To this Charlie has said, "In other words?" seeming to be honestly perplexed. It is clear to Janis at least that he is not dissembling, to use a big word that cannot properly be in her brain either. What she means to think is that Charlie is not pretending not to understand the teacher when she wants other words instead of the perfect ones he has apparently just used. Janis assumes them perfect anyway, because she doesn't herself know their meaning and she will give the benefit of the doubt to a boy in pleated short pants with his hair wet-combed and speaking clearly without giggling or mumbling. She'd like to mount Charlie Dickens, in the cloak closet if she has to, but in the bushes right outside the windows on the side of the school facing the orphanage where he lives would be better. It is not usual for a nine-year-old girl to have visions of mounting people but Janis is not a usual girl.

Charlie for his part is unusual too. He has about given up talking in class, participating in the teacher's notions of good-pupil citizenry, because it is clear she does not really like good-pupil citizenry or she would not be inhaling and sighing like that and asking for other words. Last week he said, "Crazy wooden galleries common to the backs of half a dozen houses, with holes from which to look upon the slime beneath; windows, broken and patched, with poles thrust out, on which to dry the linen that is never there; rooms so small, so filthy, so confined, that the air would seem too tainted even for the dirt and squalor which they shelter; wooden chambers thrusting themselves out above the mud, and threatening to fall into it—as some have done; dirt-besmeared walls and decaying foundations; every repulsive lineament of poverty, every loathsome indication of filth, rot, and garbage; all these ornament the banks of the ditch behind the orphanage in which I am not alone confined."

He thought he had got it about right until the teacher then said, "Can you, Charlie—" sigh—"say that in other words?"

"I'll try," he said, "but later," and sat down, because he was winded and he did not think he knew other words and he saw Janis looking at him in that way he had no words for yet.

He tried later that night to formulate words not other than those he had used to describe his mean privation but to describe the kind of looking at him Janis Joplin did. It was shy, spittlely, askance when not directly at him; *diffident*, not *shy*, he thought; perhaps *sidelong* rather than the awkward askance *when not direct; spittlely* was terse but not elegant, better to string it out with *a little gobbet of spit in the corner of her mouth as if she were hungry.* Janis did look hungry, but not in the way his peers at the orphanage looked hungry. They looked like they wanted to eat Twinkies and Janis did not look like she wanted Twinkies. Janis had this odd way of looking like an old woman sometimes, an old woman in a bed like Miss Havisham, a woman he could see in his mind, the vision of whom mystified him: he did not know who it was or why he had a name for her and could recall no one remotely like her in his life at the orphanage outside Austin, Texas.

On television Janis has seen an interview with Ray Charles that has made her interested in Ray Charles and indeed in music itself in a way that she was not interested in either Ray Charles or music before she saw the interview. Mr. Charles had on magnificent, gleaming sunglasses and rocked his head around in the air like a bird dog looking for a scent, which she knew he did because he was blind, or was supposed to be blind. Too many singers claimed to be blind for them all to be blind, she thought, but she thought Ray

Charles was probably not lying, about that. If anything made her suspicious of his blindness it was simply how good his sunglasses looked. They had gone to some trouble getting those magnificent glasses, movie-star glasses that could have been on an Italian actress if they were not there waving around like solar antennae on Mr. Charles's face. Anyway, right out of those glasses came this white sizzly blinding light into her own eyes as Mr. Charles said, "You can only make love to one woman at a time." That remark transfixed Janis. She did not know why he said it or what he had been saying or what the question was. In fact she did not know, really, what "make love to a woman" meant, let alone one at a time, but it was an idea that held a great appeal to her, clearly up there on the tree of adult knowledge. And when he said it she knew he was not lying about being blind, or about being a good singer, or about being a good singer being a good thing to be, though she did think he might be lying when he said you could only make love to one woman at a time. It sounded like he was denying something rather than just stating a fact, whatever the fact was, or whatever the denial. She could eat two apples at one time. It was dumb because they both turned a little brown as you did it but you could do it. She wondered what in fact there was you could do one of that you could not do two of at one time. She could sing two songs at one time, or five, and she did this in the bathtub and she mostly did it when she forgot lines to one song but remembered those to another but sometimes she did it for fun. Ray Charles was not on the level about that woman thing, but he was guarding his being on the level about the music thing. She thought: What if I be Ray Charles on the music thing and myself on the woman thing? I'll say you *can* make love to more than one woman at a time. She already sang very well, in the bathtub, and no one ever told her to pipe down, one reason she thought she was pretty good. José Feliciano,

Stevie Wonder, Ronnie Milsap, *and* Ray Charles? It was too much. At Blind Lemon Jefferson she gave up.

Charlie Dickens raised his hand when the teacher asked someone to describe the weather. Most of the children had merely looked out the window and begun forming the notion that it was so obvious what the weather was that the teacher was either trying to trick them or was retarded. But Charlie was the kind of kid that would step into a trick with a smile and save them all from it. Despite his weirdness, they liked him. Many smart alecks you despised but Charlie was so far out there you could not despise him for being smart. He was some kind of twilight-zone smart and he would use it, as in the present weather trick, to protect them all. "The weather?" Charlie was saying. "Implacable November weather. As much mud in the streets as if the waters had but newly retired from the face of the earth, and it would not be wonderful to meet a Megalosaurus, waddling like an elephantine lizard up Holborn Hill. Smoke lowering down from chimney-pots, making a soft black drizzle, with flakes of soot in it as big as full-grown snowflakes—gone into mourning, one might imagine, for the death of the sun. Dogs, indistinguishable in mire. Horses, scarcely better; splashed to their very blinkers. Foot passengers—"

"Charlie—"

"No, Ma'am, I can't put it in other words."

"Very well. Good job. You may be seated."

The children had been on the verge of erupting in a kind of excitement she had not seen of them before. Perhaps it was the Megalosaurus. They had helped her resist the force of Charlie Dickens before this adventure, but now it seemed they might be swinging to him, and if they wholeheartedly began to support Charlie's flights her classroom could go completely out of control.

The only child who seemed self-possessed, actually, was little Janis Joplin, who had calmly studied Charlie during his weather broadcast without squirming or giggling or otherwise beginning to vibrate to his lunacy.

Ms. Turner, as she was known to the children, was a private woman with an interest in biology that had gotten derailed. She had not gone to graduate school as she had hoped and now found herself inexplicably wrangling this small herd of mostly privileged children. She was fending off the unwanted advances of a coach from the middle school next door, a man who came round in polyester stretch pants and expensive-looking noisy athletic shoes trying to talk her into going out. This was an ordinary nuisance except that he, the coach, somehow reminded her of ordinary little Janis Joplin as she, Janis, sat there regarding the extraordinary Charlie Dickens. Ms. Turner had noticed this special regard Janis had for Charlie, and she knew what it was about, as phantasmagorical as that seemed for a child of Janis's age: she was a sexual predator as surely as Coach Leech was. Richard Leech labored under the appellation Dick Leech, which did not make his life any happier. In a kind of blinding fatalism, Ms. Turner saw that her life was already fixed in this nothingness she was in and that she was not to escape it. This vision made things paradoxically a little easier to take: she might as well relax, and settle down. Thus she had come to let Charlie Dickens, for example, go on a bit more than she once had, short of his precipitating a riot among his peers with his performances, which struck them as *tours de force* of authority thwarting or nose thumbing. They could not, she didn't think, distinguish between smart aleck and *smart*. As we have seen, she was wrong in this surmise. She could not know that the children sensed their own mundane trappedness there, as she sensed hers, and that they divined in Charlie Dickens's excesses a chance that he would by them escape and go into an orbit they themselves would be denied. He was among them a kind of early astronaut, and they liked astronauts, of any kind. She was wrong too in her apprehensions of Dick Leech's interests, because Dick Leech was as homosexual as balls were round, but Dick Leech is not within the scope of our concerns; forget him. Let's forget Ms. Turner too. Things are happening.

A girl quieter than even Janis Joplin, if that is possible, named Gail Crutchfield, who lives at the orphanage with Charlie Dickens, and who wears the most out-of-date clothes the orphanage has to hand down—today a long red plaid dress belted at the waist with a belt of the same material that makes her look like a Rockwell mother in 1940—this Gail Crutchfield, who has not opened her mouth heretofore in any enterprise in or out of class, is standing up in her desk chair and smoothing down her dress and wringing her hands nervously. She is breathing as if to prepare for something she has to say. She begins then not to talk but to sing. And to sing well. Powerfully well. At first Ms. Turner does not know the song— Hank Williams's "Your Cheating Heart"—then she is amazed that she has heard it all her life and never heard it like this. Coming from the mouth of eleven-year-old Gail Crutchfield (Gail has been held back and is older than the other children), it is spectral, not at all the bumpkin tune Ms. Turner had assumed it before.

Gail Crutchfield loses her nervousness entirely once she begins to sing. She concentrates on every note, and hits every note with authority, and uses a yodeling tremolo or vibrato where the song wants it, Ms. Turner does not know the musical term.

When she is done, the children, who have been fidgeting and making small efforts to distract her (a couple of paper balls have flown by her head), start howling derisively and clapping and booing at once, and Gail sits down, primly folding her hands and erectly staring forward, with one red-faced glance at Ms. Turner as if to apologize for interrupting the class. Gail Crutchfield seems embarrassed to have interrupted the class but not to have sung the song. She says, to whom Ms. Turner cannot tell, "Well, you *asked* me to." This is the first and only hint as to how this performance has come about in her classroom. Gail Crutchfield has not received any notice from Ms. Turner before this moment beyond that she lives with Charlie Dickens and a boy named Martin at the orphanage across the street. Ms. Turner is beginning to suspect that weird things are afoot in the room. She occasionally has this sensation: that she is on a bus and doesn't know where it is going, and hasn't even known that she is on a bus, that's how out of it she is. The phenomenon of Gail Crutchfield this morning has put her strongly in the bozo-on-the-bus frame of mind.

As he walks by the outside of the classroom after school, Charlie Dickens is whispered to loudly from the bushes under the windows the children stare out of all day. In the hedge is Janis Joplin, squatting down and hooking her finger at him. He goes in.

"Hey," Janis says, and he says, "Hi."

She kisses him wetly about his face. He is overwhelmed by her into a sitting position, legs straight out, Janis on all fours, going messily at him.

"My girl," he finally manages to say. "You have laved me as a dog so starved for affection might confuse flesh for its proper food." He is smiling because the odd displeasure of his cold wet face in the bushes outside the classroom, which should put him, he thinks, in an ill humor, is not putting him in an ill humor. Janis for her part is certain he has called her a dog, a thing she could have predicted, but notices that Charlie Dickens is smiling.

This she points out. "You are smiling, Charlie."

"Indubitably and inexplicably. The confluence of our salivas I'd not have predicted could be less than odious, but it is. This world is strange, Miss Joplin."

"You're from the Baptist Home and you are the smartest boy in school, Charlie. *That* is strange to me."

"Martin is smart in his way, and we must consider the early talent of Miss Crutchfield. What did you think of her today?"

Janis Joplin wonders how a boy who insists on wearing a trench coat and who clowns around all day, and who once ran and slid baseball style under a table when Ms. Turner was out of the room, and because under the table his feet touched a dead bird none of them had seen before that must have come in the window and died in the night stood up quickly announcing,"I killed a bird!"—Janis wonders how such a boy can be smart "in his way," in *any* way; she wonders if Charlie Dickens is not being kind as adults seem to be and want children to be instead of picking on each other as they deserve, and all of this wondering she would prefer to do, there still on her hands and knees over Charlie Dickens just like the dog he has called her, rather than think about what Gail Crutchfield did today in class, a thing that excited her and made her mad also because she has been working on something like that in the bathtub, not that song, which she knows is a Hank Williams song and not as she thinks Gail Crutchfield probably thinks a Patsy Cline song, this she can tell from the way Gail sang it, all kind of bossy instead of scared and shaky as Mr. Williams sang it. How to tell Charlie Dickens all this on her hands and knees in front of his face, the smartest boy in the world? "I have been singing in the bathtub a lot," she says finally.

Charlie Dickens regards her for a long time, just exactly as if he is thinking some large-word things up that cannot be put in other words. "You sing in the bathtub, Janis, if I may be familiar," he says at last, "and I am afraid that I wallow in a slough of despond. I am not apparently coeval with my time."

"No, you are *not*," Janis says, meaning by it nothing that Charlie can be certain of. He does not expect that she can understand him. He suspects she means that she does not deem him evil, and this is good enough and does not merit an explication of his inveterate, inscrutable, ineluctable way of speaking, since that impossible speech is primarily what he is talking about.

"I don't fit in today," he says, "but you do, as shy as you seem, and as troubled. Your desperation is within reach of its targets, I mean, Miss Joplin. Mine is not. Mine is well lost. I feel, in other words"—they both giggle—"very old somehow, and you are very young. My desperations are behind me, as odd as that may sound, and yours are ahead of you, yet to be discovered."

This relaxes Janis. She can see herself kissing him again, and singing in the tub, and singing standing on her own desk chair, showing them the weak and shaky and real way to sing songs. "I want to have big boobs and blond hair," she says.

Charlie Dickens shakes his head ever so slightly, like a wise man. Like some grandfather in the cutest short pants who lives in the Baptist Home! Janis thinks.

"You might want large breasts, Janis, but you do not want blond tresses that are fine and flaxen because, well, it is a hard matter to put delicately, but men do not want, in spite of all their proclamations to the contrary, to see Johnny Winter down there— excuse me, I mean Edgar. They do not wish to see Edgar Winter in the perturbations of their rut when they are weak with need and not ready to see Edgar Winter. Down there."

"Down where?"

"In other words, in your pants."

"Charlie, you are too weird. Who is Edgar Winter?"

"You will learn who he is. You will make a mark."

· "You are so smart, you will be famous, Charlie."

"No, quick child. I think not. It is improper, or at least it would play verily at the edges of the field of impropriety, for me to burden you with my troubles. They are vast. As I have intimated, I am an old man, somehow, ill-befitting this age, and my age. This will precipitate in me a long degrade of faculties, what is called I believe a nervous breakdown. You will have one of these too, but your taper burns at the other end, as it were, the correct end. Mine burns from the base."

Janis giggled at this speech, and with it Charlie began to struggle to his feet and Janis let him get up. In two months' time third grade would be over, she would have kissed Charlie Dickens two more times, and he would disappear over the summer and not be in school in Austin, Texas, for the fourth grade. She would discover the books written by Charles Dickens, hear Grace Slick tell Johnny Carson, "I would have blond hair and big boobs," when he asked her, "If you could do it all over again, what would you do different?", see both Johnny and Edgar Winter play their guitars in Port Arthur, sing herself well beyond the bathtub, and never properly be as much in love as she was the day Charlie Dickens told her all that he told her in the bushes outside the classroom, his cute boy knees and his difficult man mouth.

Mrs. Fiberung

The odds that Mrs. Fiberung were to retire that day after thirty years of service and set her car on fire inadvertently and narrowly preserve the Girl Scout cookies from its trunk and mosey on home eating them with great satisfaction and get there and find her son cavorting in the swimming pool with a girl, when she had theretofore thought him uninterested in girls, and a letter of foreclosure on the house, and two lizards either fighting or mating on the kitchen table, and a volleyball net inexplicably strung in the backyard, and a complete inability to recall her husband and the nastiness of the divorce, and a strange and harmless man slumped in a corner of her garage, whom she shooed away without calling the police, which was probably against principles of bourgeois suburban protocol, was incalculable. Were incalculable. The odds. Who wished to calculate anything these days anyway?

Who broached the notion of odds and their calculability? Her car was on fire, her son was in the pool with a girl, lizards were going at it on the table, the cookies were good, she felt better about life in general than she had in years. This is a gift horse not to look in the mouth or the rear end either for that matter. Let it be lame. Accept it.

She called her son in and his girlfriend and they stood there apprehensively dripping on the carpet, shivering a little, their shoulders narrowed under their towels, which were draped over them. "Cavorting in the pool like that with no one here to chaperone you will make the neighbors talk," she said. "Go up to your room." The girl looked from her to her son incredulously and then followed her son, who had already started up, to his room.

Mrs. Fiberung hoped they took full advantage of this chaperoning. She was an expert militant chaperone and believed in the full exercise of the seditious power a chaperone was in position to wield. While she had thought her son homosexual she had of course maintained there was nothing really wrong in that, but she now discovered a very strong sense of relief in herself, almost a joy, a high that she sought to confirm and prolong and deepen by sending the two of them to a private room. They were nearly pickled by the chlorinated water anyway, she had noticed.

She put on a trench coat her husband had left and modeled in it before a full-length mirror, looking like a spy. Some odd words and ideas came nearly to her mind that she could not completely grasp or assemble: *furtivclature* was one of them. She took that thought out to the pool and got in a chaise, still in the coat, with a drink, and found that *furtivclature* had shifted to *numcnboles* or *numenholus*. These entities in her head, whatever they were, suggested to her the idea that she wanted to become a radically different person from that she had been to this point in her life. Was that possible, or was it only an idea that everyone entertained once in a while and, like these oddball words, could not quite really possess or effect? Did the urge just not leave you, like these new words, incomplete and unformed and undefined? Was it not the case, for example, that in launching into a "new you" you typically got about as far as drinking by your pool in a spy coat in the middle of the afternoon and hoping your son was seizing the day upstairs in his bedroom? Was it not more likely that the two of them would be regarding her now through the slit blinds of that room and speculating as to what was wrong with her, and that soon she would abandon the poolside chaise and return the coat to its hanger and be back exactly to herself after the girl went home properly unmolested?

I suggest we leave Mrs. Fiberung upon the horns of her little dilemma on the grounds that she is as capable as we are of solving what are, after all, her trivial problems. We have problems of our own we might be better advised to inspect. To the extent that they too are trivial, we might well advise our ownself to abjure them too. To hell with Mrs. Fiberung and her little problems, and to hell with us and our little problems, and let us get on with it.

The odd volleyball net is before us beside the pool that Mrs. Fiberung has quit. Husbands do leave, boys do stray, girls do play, the *Wide World of Sports* will cover about anything. Buttocks. Buttocks in spandex. Before the buttocks develop that large-curd cottage-cheese dimpling, one of the saddest things on earth and one of God's chief oversights. On the other hand, the buttocks before the curding is one of His proudest moments and indeed one of the signal arguments for His existence. To see Him working his way toward the human buttock, whether with the hand of the Darwinian selector or not, traveling from the hairy hind of quadrupeds to the fulgent, obscene turquoise and carmine noise of the baboon's operatic ass to the smooth, domed, cleaved, in-the-beginning firm-as-Jell-O and perfect-for-spanking human buttocks is to see a great mind at work, and to place the buttocks in that relation to the shitty rump of an ox or to the cloaca of the slithering beast is not less than placing the sun in relation to a planet. Because of the butt, God exists. I have a butt, or had a butt, therefore I am the son of God.

Gift

Put on these Indian flyer things here.

What are you talking about?

These.

Put them where?

On your ears, I guess.

Have you lost your mind?

No. Why?

I am not putting those on my ears.

I think that's what they're for.

You think those are earrings?

What else are they?

They look more like bagpipes, or porcupines. Put *them on your ears*.

I got them for you.

Well take them back.

I can't.

Why not?

The Indians said they would kill me if I tried to exchange a purchase. Tribal law allows this, owing to the long history of broken treaties, etc.

The earrings are moving.

Good God.

Those *are* porcupines. They sold you drugged porcupines. You are a fucking idiot, even before you announced I was to *wear* them.

How was I to know what they are? All I know about porcupines is that they eat buildings.

That is probably why the Indians won't exchange them for something that does not eat buildings.

Why didn't the Indians just kill them?

Instead of get money from you to take them away?

Yes.

I don't know. That's a hard one.

I couldn't see them well. They were half in the box, in tissue paper.

Something in a Dell computer box, weighing forty pounds, they tell you is earrings, and you buy it.

They said it was some kind of "flyer things," they mumbled, I thought they meant some kind of ceremonial headdress, not mere earrings, I don't know.

I think this is a transitional relationship.

What is?

You and me. You and I.

Transitional?

Yes. Crossing.

Into what?

Into not a relationship.

Because I bought you some earrings that turn out to be live animals? You regard that as an *infraction*?

That you expect me to strap twenty-pound balls of deadly quills to my head, yes, that is an infraction.

I don't expect it now that I see what they are.

That makes it even worse. You'd be somehow less stupid if you drugged *me* now and tied these things to my head.

You fly off the handle at the least provocation. I think you are right. The relationship is ABC. I will find a woman who does not freak because you buy her a surprising gift.

I'll have a lot of fun telling people about my ex who bought me porcupine earrings, *whole porcupine* earrings.

A gross distortion. They'll know you are crazy.

I won't be able to deny it, for having been with you up to that point.

Your whole life will become a fabric of lies if you start saying shit like that.

Shit like what?

Forget it. I bet these guys make good pets if you can keep them from eating the house. I think I'll ride out to the rez and thank the Indians profusely. They'll be laughing at me and it will be perfect. I'm in a new zone. We're all stupid, finally, baby doll, so you might as well get free in the deep end. Where you can maneuver.

Sisters

You won't believe what Steve did yesterday.

Steve who?

Steve Peanutbrain.

What?

He bought two porcupines and expected me to wear them as earrings.

So? Did you?

I did not. They weighed twenty pounds apiece and started moving. For starters.

Ralph the boinkologist last week invited a squirrel to breakfast in our house and fed it eggs and jelly at the table. I said what the hell was going on and Ralph said, "Hey, this guy went to the fifth grade." The squirrel looked up from the industry of chewing through a jelly pack and tipped his hat to me. Ralph had put a hat on him. He was the size of a small bear.

Maybe he *had* been to fifth grade.

That's what I'm thinking about then. I asked why Ralph didn't give the guy some jelly from the jar and he said he'd already been through that with the guy. The squirrel had found the jelly pack at a picnic and wanted to eat it and he wanted to open it himself. We watched him nibble around the jelly pack. He dropped it and retrieved it from the floor and was back in the chair with unbelievable quickness. His hat fell off and Ralph put it back on his head.

So all in all you had a better time of it than I did with Steve offering me porcupine earrings.

I guess I did.

When will it ever end?

What?

Life, I guess.

Has it begun?

I think it has.

Well if it has, it is going to end soon enough. We don't have much in the way of prospects. Our husbands are bringing rodents into the house for odd purposes. They arguably are not of sound mind.

We are with them, so we are not of sound mind either.

Would we be any worse off, really, had you strapped the porcupines to your head and had I had a bite with the squirrel at my own table?

I'd be worse off, you might have gotten away with it. I'd be in the hospital.

People must talk about us.

Yes. And tell me, do you want to hear what they have to say?

No.

Life can go on as it must as long as I do not have to listen to people *talk*.

Maybe this is what Steve and Ralph are onto. They aren't exactly out there soliciting the approbation of people or listening to them. Steve finds it funny that the Indians think they duped him.

What Indians?

The Indians who sold him the porcupine earrings, telling him apparently they were ceremonial headdress.

That's funny.

That's why he bought them, I think. I maybe overreacted.

I think you did.

Maybe you were a little short with the fifth-grade squirrel.

Maybe I was.

Maybe we owe some apologies.

I think we do. Let's have a cookout.

Steve's pretty mad.

We'll wear teddies, like a Hefner scene. Or I have this very sexy old-fashioned tan two-piece. Get the squirrel a case of jelly packs. What do the porcupines eat?

Treated plywood, I think.

We have that.

I really don't like people, you know that?

We are sisters!

I will try a little P.T. plywood myself.

The Lord is my shepherd. Shall I want?

You shan't. What do you mean, tan two-piece?

It's like flesh-colored. Hideous. Very sexy in 1959.

There is something so noble about cheap, bad clothing.

The whole business of being a refugee. What is more noble than that?

Are we refugees?

We are. We are armchair refugees, but still refugees.

We have refuged, or *been* refuged . . . how does the word work?

I do not know. I only know that it is the club you want to be in, short of starving to death. If you are not in the club of the refugee then you are with the oppressors, the people who listen to themselves talk.

The people who dismiss your bathing suit as out of fashion.

Who scoff at squirrels to breakfast and porcupine earrings.

We better be careful. We have a narrow line to toe.

That we do, sister Yanniling. I feel a Pop-Tart hankering coming on.

Perhaps South America

The slender means of tying up the anaconda were in the *Manual of Bevels*. We did not have the manual. We had no idea what "bevels" meant. But it was a manual; we thought it was our survival manual. We had lost it, we thought. We were on the edge of a village, we surmised. The people looking at us seemed to be villagers, and behind them seemed to be a village. We had debated all morning what we were. insurgents or counterinsurgents, mercenaries or government troops, rebels or establishment. There was a proposition on the floor that a group of us go to one end of the village and pretend to be drunk and say "Danny Ortega" and see what happened, and another group go to the other end of the village and pretend to be drunk and say "U.S. Marines" and see what happened. No one wanted to affix himself to either group. It was thought that we might actually be drunk and need not pretend. We had had nothing to drink, we thought, but still it seemed tenable that we were drunk. We were not hiding from the villagers as caution might have suggested. We had no weapons or any other signs of militariness about us but several of us were convinced we were somehow on the violent side of the fence, if there was a fence down here, wherever we were. It was the vaguest feeling, this notion that we were brutes, and no one was unhappy with it even if he doubted those who argued so hard with no evidence that we were soldiers of some sort.

The one certainty was the big anaconda that we thought we had once had instructions to tie up. Two of us spoke with certainty of the *Manual of Bevels* and the rest of us felt vaguely familiar with the title and did not outright dispute that in it, if the book existed, there might well be instructions for neutralizing a large anaconda. The anaconda was, however, very passive. He looked about two hundred pounds and as if he could easily down a goat and no one really saw the need to tie him up.

Someone said he thought the anaconda could talk, and no one disputed even this. We were not certain of much. A good-looking girl came by and smiled and no one knew what to do about it. Four or five of us proposed we sleep some more. This sounded like a good idea but we were nervous. Fenster Ludge said he would urinate on anyone who went to sleep, and four or five of us instantly napped out. The rest of us watched Fenster, who did nothing. Fenster was perhaps a person we knew to be all bluster. This was the most we thought we knew at that point in the ordeal.

We wondered if we could get scrambled eggs from someone in the village. They had chickens running the range and the eggs might be very good, we thought. We came, we thought, if we thought free-range eggs good, from a place where the eggs were not very good because they might be not free-range. We could be Marines after all. "Yes," Fenster said, "those are not Frank Perdue chickens." Someone asked what he meant and he said he had no idea, but several others said that what he said felt as familiar as the *Manual of Bevels* and tying up an anaconda.

"I am tired of this shit," Larry said. "The manual is in the plane, the plane crashed, we walked out of there with amnesia, our guns are in the plane, fuck the anaconda, fuck Danny Ortega, I am going to get that girl." Hear, hear! some of us cheered, but no one, including Larry, moved. Then Larry started taking off his clothes. No one paid much attention. Larry started inspecting his clothes closely, as if he did not quite comprehend what they were. He had them off and the rest of us also regarded them as curiosities, rather like a word that has been repeated many times until it seems perfectly odd and meaningless. Yet it did not occur to us to so inspect our own clothes or that our own might be curious also. When he had reached the point in his examination of his clothes that their meaninglessness itself seemed meaningless, Larry put them back on, agreeably shaking his head. Like the odd and meaningless word we agree to continue to use in spite of its nonsense, the clothes had a utilitarian value. Every one of us imagined the anaconda in Larry's clothes. We looked at Larry and at the anaconda and back at Larry and then at each other and all laughed, all clearly on the current of the exact same idea. Of this we were certain, and nothing else.

Fenster seemed to nap out and awoke in an agitated state saying his wife was leaving him. Larry said, "Fenster, that is what wives do." This had a calming effect on Fenster, and on the rest of us. Conversation developed then that explored the wife-specific lacunae of our situation. We did not know, for example, that Fenster had a wife, nor did he, finally, know that he had a wife. Larry did not know if he had one. None of us knew anything about wives, our own or others'. This gap fit with the other gaps. The wives, we decided, were at the crash site, or at the altar, or they had repudiated us entire, perhaps before we had met them. We had wives but we had never met them. This is the way it always is and always will be, we decided. We were fairly secure and comfortable after this resolution of the wife lacuna.

A rain of parrots came down on us. Bright turquoise birds with orange heads alighted on us. Some of us had two and some up to five birds. They did no violence to us, and no defecating, which we discovered were our two chief anticipations if a large bird were to land on you. The beaks of these things were as large as cow horns. We discovered that we were, festooned with parrots in this way, the only colorful spot in the landscape of the village. The village was a drab black and white, like a movie before Ted Turner got to it, someone said. Someone else said, "Get out of here." Someone else said, "That girl who came by, smiling, who Larry said he was going to get, what a hound dog he is, never caught a rabbit and he ain't no friend of mine, that girl had a red mouth." This seemed to have been so. We concluded that the parrots and the girl's mouth had color. The rest, to include us, was bleached out, or never filled in. To say, we did not know if our condition of colorlessness represented a removal of a quality or if colorfulness was an addition to a basal state of colorlessness. "We'd better be content," Fenster said, "to just be cautious empiricists, given . . ."

"Right," Larry said, "Whoever said I ain't nothin' but a hound dog, fuck you."

"You two should fight."

"Right," Larry said. "Who said that shit about me?"

No one could remember. Whoever said it was not afraid to confess but he was as unable as the rest of us to recall if he said it. We could not identify him partly because we could not remember what happened two minutes ago and partly, we thought, because we did not know our own names, beyond Fenster and Larry, who, having known names, suddenly looked to us, and even to themselves, very suspicious, as if they were plants or spies or some other stripe of interloper among us normal guys. We decided to have a roll call. We gave ourselves five minutes to recall or make up the name we would go by. We agreed to abide by whatever we came up with, as you agree to sit the entire semester or year in the same seat you first choose in some classrooms.

"Fenster."

"Larry."

"Fuck you two guys. Bonhomie."

"Travis."

"Turk."

"Tork."

"Sam."

"Turl."

"Teal."

"Tod."

Okay. There were ten of us. That made things handy. We might as well use a base-10 numbering system if we got around to that.

When it was full dark, the parrots removed to the trees, we longed for girls like the smiling one to come out of the village and visit us but they did not, and airplanes rolled in issuing thunder and lightning, black-and-white brimstone and fire. This, we knew, should have frightened us, but it did not. We did not take cover. It would be a better learning experience to observe the damnation with our full attention. Our full attention would be compromised if we were to scramble under, say, pieces of tin and culverts and banana trees. So we sat there as if at a noisy picnic. No one got hurt.

The village went up in flames. The villagers danced in silhouette against the orange mayhem.

Fenster yelled, "Take me down to funky town!"

Larry said, "Shut up."

Tork said, "Teal, that is the gayest name I ever heard."

Teal said, "I don't dispute it."

"Look at *that*," Turk said.

The woman with the red lips flew by on a flying carpet doing this Egyptian dance thing, her palms pressed together and her head doing that side-to-side thing. It was a joke dance, a cartoon of some sort of cultural irony, we thought. We think we thought this. It was a big thought, unsafe for empiricists, and difficult to entertain even in calm tranquility, and we were not in calm tranquility, we who were being bombed.

"She's goofing," Bonhomie said. "She is not doing that as a serious expression of herself."

"What I want to know," Turl said, "is is that number serious *any*where? I mean how does someone presume to know how Egyptians *moved*?" This was the position we held. She flew on into the jungle, into darkness not illuminated by the exploding ordnance, her bright red mouth decreasing and disappearing like a taillight.

We awaited her return, and we knew that awaiting her return was at once what we could not avoid and what would paralyze us and doom us. There was nothing for it. Paralysis and doom and belief in something better than paralysis and doom is all we are given, men with assumed names and occasional parrots and bluster and bad memories in a black-and-white landscape. We were hound dogs who would never catch a rabbit and we were no friends of ours.

Confidence

I don't think, today, that I think much or have much to say. But let's sit here and see. That is a compound verb. I do not have a compound eye, or brain. Some people do, the latter, some insects the former. They look menacing and intelligent. The dragonfly in particular looks like a small but lethal military unit.

Now I am thinking of turds, small and lethal non-military units. It is snowing so I do not have to go to the gym. I should want to go to the gym, and maybe I do, and maybe I will, go.

The snow looks like blown rice. I am new to snow. I like it when it resembles popcorn and floats back up, and thwartwise, at points on its way down. I wish I had a place to plant five thousand trees on. Blue trees, perhaps. I would like it most if they were from seed in good rows about five inches high, no bigger than annuals, blue, in perfect grid array, a tree carpet. One of the benefits of living alone is unguarded farting.

•

Another is no one watching when you sleep, and when you don't. You may pursue whatever is mindless until you yourself are tired of it. You may control the density of stuff in the refrigerator. If you find your fly open, you may leave it so for a bit. No rush.

Lonely and a little chilly, I go down to the Thumb and Thumb Lingua Spanka Academy for some human intercourse and convivialismatic rompromp. Earl Thumb gouges my eye not five feet in the door, and Wonka Thumb comes over with a broom and pretends to sweep me, trash on the floor, back out the door. "You fuckers," I say, and Earl is at the computer telling me I am not paid up, and Wonka drops a knee on my stomach and hisses viciously, "I bet you think you need a *woman!*" He begins outright beating me with the broom as Earl hands me a dues bill. It's always good here, always fun. A child runs naked screaming through the room with a smile on his face, looking for approval, and disappears into the locker room. "Who's that?"

"That's a boy we are going to adopt," Wonka says, "as soon as we decide what to rename him. Negotiations are underfoot."

"Don't you think Eel is a good name?" Earl says.

I say I do or I don't, it depends on the boy's character. If he is an Eel, well then maybe. You have to wait it out, as with a dog. "Great character-warping injustice is done at the maternity ward with the birth certificates," I say.

"Eel Thumb," Wonka says.

"Eel Thumb," Earl says.

"He belongs to one of Earl's ex-wives."

"Can you lend me ten dollars?" Earl says, apparently to me. They want to buy supplies to make pull-candy to entertain the boy, and I contribute ten dollars.

I go on my way, feeling better.

•

At the used-car dealership around the corner a fat salesman is leaned into the open hood of a car throwing onions from it without regard to where they fly. "There's going to be *hell to pay* when I catch the *fuckers* did this," he says, still in there, addressing no one but himself. I cop two whole nice onions.

The zoo has about a 65% occupancy rate as near as I can tell. It is finally better to determine a cage outright empty than to contain a moribund specimen of this or that, and 35% empties makes for a mood-lightening visit. The concessions are all closed, which also helps. The little train is not running. No geese are around the lake. The action is limited to a BFI truck arming up dumpsters and banging them into itself and setting them back down. The bull elephant gets a boner standing in his compound by himself. It pulses down to the ground, looking part leg, part trunk, touches dirt, and then throbs shrinking back up into himself. Fine day at the zoo all around.

The helicopter factory, where I am said to work, has an area of rotor blades that I love. It is two acres of stacked, carefully packed alloy blades that look like giant slender knives, sashimi knives for whales, say. The blades are coated with Teflon-ey stuff in subtle yellows and grays that makes them just reek of *well-made*. I like to feel the coatings, thump and pat and stroke the blades. I object to wearing my hard hat and in a stupid protest have pasted a nude Ridgid Tool calendar girl inside it, distorting her as I am told the figures are distorted on the ceiling of the Sistine Chapel. It is hard to tell in fact that it is a naked woman inside my hat. Nonetheless, this announces somehow that the hat and my wearing it I regard as absurd. I would never have an upright and intelligible picture of such a woman on, say, the door of my locker.

Not having pets is depressing, but having pets is a troublesome prospect. So I hold steady, without.

I had a wife but she ran off and married the President of the United States. Her ultimate choice of mate subjected me to an unusual level of scrutiny from our government. I was at first regarded as part of her background, as something about which all should be known, and then I was regarded as a potential threat to her and to the President. I have assured three branches of federal law bureagents that I am happy for her, and for Him. They almost believe me sometimes. A brown car is parked at all times on my street with one or two bureagents in it. The best I can do. I do not overtly notice them, which they prefer. You may not, I have discovered, offer baked goods to your stakeout men without causing them some paperwork they would prefer not having to do. I remember when they explained all that to me ("off the record") saying, "Gee whiz." That's all I could come up with. Not Holy cow, not Boy oh boy, not Dang, not Darn, not Fuck that, but Gee whiz!

I want to paint something but I don't know what. Something around me needs a bold new redness or blueness and everything would be better. It will have to be a subtle hue—an auburny red, a blue with purple and aqua lurking in it like the surface of a fish, say—and it will have to be applied with consummate care so that it looks professional, not grubbed on in a hurry by someone who shops at malls and watches a lot of cable TV. This new red or blue thing around me will have to look like it came from West Germany or Sweden and has consultants behind it. It will make me or anyone else near it feel assured of things, as if, say, one could certainly afford at this moment to eat a piece of candy with no compunction. And do some exercise. Offer an apology where none might be strictly necessary or anticipated—not a big deal, mind you, but just a sign that one is sensitive. Yes. Paint.

If Greta and Kitty come over, I will make love to them simultaneously. They don't like this particularly, but they like the alternative less. When they come over together, I feel that they have made a choice in this respect. The difficulty is ardor, specifically with showing it. Showing ardor is regarded a good thing usually, but not when a third party is idly standing by waiting her turn. So things get rather unnaturally subdued, as if there are children in the next room, say, when in fact it is a woman who ostensibly approves of everything going on sitting, or lying, right next to you.

Kitty is the younger and the prettier of the two sisters and she usually defers to Greta. She has the resources, mental and physical, that allow her to wait. Then Greta watches us with a sad and somber aspect, her lip almost trembling, and sometimes I am nearly unmanned by her expression, but Kitty's insistent enthusiasm and fine form and gleaming eye, winking at me or Greta or both of us, keeps me to the task. They grew up on Aruba and are cosmopolitan girls. I would not expect behavior like theirs from most bona fide American sisters, unless they were from deep in the South, say Kershaw, South Carolina. The cosmopolitanism of the true sticks is huge and always surprising.

I saw some Marine recruits working their way through what is called a Confidence Course on Parris Island. It resembles an obstacle course, and whether Confidence is a euphemism or whether there is another course called an Obstacle Course I do not know. You would not think the Marines given to euphemism, but they are peculiar in their psychologies there. The boys were not prime physical specimens and from the way they were moving I believe them to have been made sore, deeply sore, by their drills.

They looked to have great difficulty climbing over the equivalent of a sawhorse. I believe they were bone sore. The Marines wanted them to move when they felt they could not. This, I suppose, engenders confidence. I would like to apply myself seriously to an endeavor that would make my life a serious, confident proposition, not a whimsical one, but so far I cannot.

When you break a tennis-racket string, do you take it to the shop for restringing, or should you have bought a spare racket and continue that day with the spare? On the one hand the second racket means you have taken yourself and time seriously, on the other it means you have taken playing a game more seriously than keeping thy money in thy pocket, a Biblical injunction. So how do you tell what to do? This I cannot discover. I am not wise. I can but walk around, greeting the friends I do not have—Hi Earl, hi Wonka, hi Eel, you now Greta, now you Kitty—seeing the animals in their cages and not in their cages, the geese on the lake and not.

Change of Life

I could not decide whether purchasing new clothes for the entire family was better than buying these new Government Cookie Flyers. Our life would be very exciting with new cookie flyers, not to mention patriotic and support the cause, etc. We had not seen the new Government Cookie Flyers but we had heard they were sharp and well engineered, perhaps even made in Germany though of course that was being withheld, if they were of foreign manufacture. Whereas new clothes would have made us fashionable and comfortable and sporty in a more obvious if short-lived way. We'd look good, but the new cookie flyers might actually *do* us more good. I just could not decide.

Nothing was helping me in this decision. You heard that thousands had bought the cookie flyers but you did not see anyone with one or using one. It was like Reagan voters. But you did see people with natty clothes on, all the time, and they did not look unhappy, that their being in new clothes meant they had foregone the patriotic route and not bought a cookie flyer but the natty clothes they were openly modeling instead. Of course they might have more money than we did and might have bought a cookie flyer also and have it at home and then be out feeling good in new clothes to boot, for all I knew. Nothing was any help in trying to decide. I tried to talk even to the dog about it, thinking at first that a dog would favor a new cookie flyer over our suddenly appearing in clothes with strange smells or no smells to him, but when he sat there looking at me dumbly as I asked him if we should get a cookie flyer or clothes, I realized he was not going to tell me.

There is a guy out in the parking lot right now who I believe is unemployed, who drives a car with a missing trunk lock away from and back to the apartment several times a day, always smoking, and now he is changing tires on the car, and I thought my life superior to his until now. Out there now with a nice chrome wheel and a cigarette he looks to have more on the ball by far than I do in here in the cookie-flyer vs. new-clothes quandary. He's a cross between Kris Kristofferson and Randall "Tex" Cobb.

I should just go out there and beat him up. That would break some logjam in here, or some ice, or something. You might not think there is a connection, or that my quandary would be served a laxative were I to without seeming provocation whip the ass of a contented layabout working on wheels and smoking, but it most assuredly would, I sense it, logically I can't help you any. We are not in the zone of logic, we are in the zone of cookie flyers and deadbeats and indecision racking our entire mortal coil and time, what little we have of it, on earth. If you do not already divine what I am talking about, there's nothing for it, no explaining this. It would take poetry, or religion, to get through. I don't have those. I don't want those. I want to know only whether to get the new Government Cookie Flyer or the clothes, period.

And now that you have your Government Cookie Flyer—
you will want two or three more, to be sure, but one is a start—
you shall take it from the box. Pull those brass staples out with
these pliers. These are Klein, very nice, now (finally) available at
Sears. I worry about Sears. Cut the tape, set your utility knife at a
sixteenth, or if you are using your pocket knife you know how to
pinch the blade exposing only the tip. Cut the length across and
now the two sides all the way, describing an H, very gratifying
somehow, like a goalpost—open the box, score a touchdown! Now
the whole business will slide out. Pull the Styrofoam braces off.
Now everything is bagged in a nice gray plastic, some of it actually
shrink-wrapped onto the large parts. Snip those and listen for the
vacuum as air enters the Cookie Flyer. Unpeel everything, lay out
the parts, get the exploded view, assemble. The Germans (reveal
this to no one) supply a tube of Loctite but we prefer not to use
it. We keep a dedicated 5/16" nut driver tied to the Flyer and like
to manually check torques continuously. It helps us stay in touch
with this fine machine, we feel, and we feel better in touch with a
fine machine.

Sweep up the chips, put them in one or two of the plastic bags,
put the Styrofoam braces back in the box in the correct orientation,
tape the box lightly back up, put it in the attic or basement.
Sometimes these days one is asked to ship in original container but
also sometimes in a new container the warranty server provides,
you do not ever know in advance, so we'll have you save the box.

Behold the brand-new Government Cookie Flyer on your floor.
Congratulations. Your life has changed, it is safe to say. Very safe
to say. One's life changes all the time, one might say, or it does not
change all the time, another might say, and both might be right.
When we caught the magnificent catfish in the muddy Brazos and
ate it, and can still see that shiny gray fish fighting on that shiny red

mud, so handsome, so strong, undone by his appetite for a chicken gizzard, we might say our life changed, or we might not. But with the Government Cookie Flyer on your floor, your life has changed.

The moment I touched the Flyer my life did change. I saw to the core of adult capitalist life, what constitutes the Highest Good: IT IS THE MOMENT YOU INDUCE OTHERS TO GIVE YOU A LOT OF MONEY FOR SOMETHING THAT DID NOT COST YOU MUCH TO SUPPLY. This I now know is the only lasting thrill—not meeting a woman or having good drugs or securing a good job or car or seeing God or whatever. The thrill that the Big Boys are about is in duping for cash. I took the Flyer out and let one fly right by the idiot mechanic in the parking lot as he performed his endless machinations on his beloved car. He stood up from the wheel he sat on while studying a brake drum, stamped out his cigarette, advanced on me with the built-in menace in his gait, and said he would give me the pink slip to the car at that moment, and do me a barbecue that night, and invite his wife's sister over for me to meet, that she was newly divorced and lonely and hot, if I would give him the Flyer. I said no way with such certainty that he stopped lighting the new cigarette he was about to light and kicked me squarely in the groin. He looked at me a moment on the ground, lit the cigarette, and returned to the car.

Now things are so clear. When I see any government functionary, say the Secretary of State, or Defense, speaking ostensibly about this diplomatic matter or that military matter, respectively, I can now divine the truth underlying the positions. The man speaking, were he not in Government service, would be a major CEO pulling a multimillion-dollar salary, an income he has chosen to forego for the nonce in order to protect thousands of other multimillion-dollar salaries, and on this his integrity depends, if not his life. His colleagues the Big Boys watch him serve and protect, and they hold open a position for him when he is done with the sacrifice. They are the high priests in the world's most successful religion. Every store is a church, every ad a psalm, every entrepreneur a preacher, every buyer a believer. And it all rests on a solid spiritual principle: since material goods are insignificant and money crass, why not always give a little more than the material is worth? What harm there? The Government Cookie Flyer makes this abundantly clear, inadvertently I'm sure. But a machine of this genius has unpredictable powers, few limitations, a broad adaptability for perhaps unlimited uses. Among them— and this application I am certain was not intentional, for it strikes at the heart of a large market just now, if not the largest market on earth—is that I need not use a phone. I may think of a call and let the Cookie Flyer fly, and the matter is done, not one dial tone, fiber optic, roam, message, beep, vibration, satellite involved. The called party strangely knows the import of my call and communicates his or her response on the return fly, coterminous with his receipt of my call. Thus, in effect, I can communicate with everyone on earth, just sitting here, sometimes without their being aware of it. Just a side benefit of owning the Government Cookie Flyer, like a small potato chip, or *piece* of a chip, on the plate of a very large and ultimately satisfying meal. With the Flyer I called my doctor about the embarrassing prospect of having him inspect my throbbing testicles and learned that only an over-the-counter anti-inflammatory is indicated, ice if I want to amuse myself with frozen parts, and that any permanent damage, unlikely, will be in the positive direction of free and non-surgical vasectomy, which I needed anyway. I have put an ice pack in my shorts and eaten some aspirin and flown a call to my malicious neighbor yet working on his car, asking him if he is absolutely certain of his tattooed wife's fidelity, sometimes a problem with a woman so much younger than an aging, balding, overweight husband and with a woman so goddamned good-looking, a fact he overlooks, has he taken a good look at her lately? The answer that came back, as he sat staring at the wheel bearings, was No, bullshit, and he got up and went in the house, from which I now hear noise, very satisfying as I adjust the ice cubes better.

Cries For Help, Various

Cry for Help from France

My toilet is from Paris. A coward is full of bluster about living well. A coward is terrified of even being alive. He may be also afraid—and this is congruent with the more popular visions of cowardice—of the opposite, both in its extreme, final expression (death), and in its less acute expressions (injury). But fear of injury or death, running from battles or fistfights, etc., is just shallow cowardice; in fact it may not be cowardice at all. It may be mere anxiety, and usually rather rational at that. Who is to be faulted for preferring not to have his nose broken or not to die on the ground in the dirt without any painkillers or a girl to wipe one's brow? No, that is cosmetic cowardice. True cowardice would embrace a broken nose or the spectacle of one's guts flying while being afraid of buying a new car or getting married or having a child or changing jobs or selecting this coat over that coat or eating at a restaurant that is too expensive or one that is not expensive enough. A true coward knows the phrase *Go for it* and he deigns not go for it. Going for it scares him to death. He is so far from going for it that he does not even conceive what is to be gone for. This is why he does not perceive, usually, that he is a coward. Excuse me, I've been writing this, just now, and I'll admit to bearing down a bit to try to get my meaning correct, and clear if it is correct, and I fancy at this point it is clear but not yet correct—when a fat boy skipped by on the street, trying to skip, so uncoordinated that it lent the impression that his bones were soft, or even possibly bending. A goofy, happy, or let us say perhaps an unhappy boy trying to be happy, badly skipping down a sunny street in France. It is likely, in my imagination, at first, that this boy is not a coward. Then I immediately correct: he is likely not *yet* a coward. He does not know. He is still at the level of trying to see if his overfed and underused soft body will respond to a command he gives it, which command should be fun to obey. He has gone around the corner, gone with his early unconscious exploration into cowardice, and I now sit here with my later investigations. I am at a good oak table. I have coffee. It is quiet in this nice house in France. Send me some money, you people. I am just like Robert Crumb, who has retired to south France, except he can draw.

Another day, still here. Another fat boy has manifested. He tapped on a window on the side of the house and I steered him to the front door. He had a laminated card identifying himself, avec photo, currently dated, as a collector for the handicapped. He was very relaxed, made a joke about someone going down the street. I explained that I do not speak well, and his apparent answer was, Well, it's for the handicapped, what need is there for speech or further comprehension? I gave him a small handful of change, he manifested momentary disappointment, then quickly assented that it was good, C'est bon. Probably legitimate. It has upset the day of the coward. Giving a small amount of change to a probably legitimate undertaking, or to a possibly illegitimate undertaking, is perfect cowardice. Deciding the venture was real or fraudulent either way and giving nothing, slamming the door, or deciding it was maybe real or even fraudulent and giving a goodly sum, flank the act of cowardice and have about them vapors of courage. You will not find me on those flanks. I am in the very center of fear and being small. A fat boy on the streets of France knows it.

And what would you say, Sir, to the chance we might mount a draft horse in chain mail and swarp down the enemy in rows like wheat?

Aye, bonnie good that, let's do, and then let's try not to dissect the swarping of our fellows and find less in it than heroism. Will we be able to manage that?

I am only thy valet, Sire. I can put thee on the mount, I cannot determine how thou ridest.

Cry for Help from Home

My grandfather kept bees. I never saw him at this enterprise and do not know precisely how I know that he pursued it. I have had the urge to have bees myself but so far have not procured a single bee. My father was a gambler. I think that was his essence. In high school he hustled pool halls, in WWII he joined the Marines before being drafted, in life he struck out in entrepreneurial ventures and real-estate developments. In his last hours he escaped the house and walked to the 7-Eleven and bought a lottery card, got lost and tired on the way home, and was brought to the door by two women who wanted to know if they could keep him. They had found him sitting on their low garden wall, they found him charming, and they brought him home. I have never gambled on a thing in my life.

Cry For Help from the Theater of Love

Jogging along lightly, nude, I encounter some Vermont-hiker-looking folk before I can cut off the road so say, "Finally tried out some *really light* backpacking ha!" and cut for the house, crossing the porch on which I had not noticed the preponderance of trash before, but I had only crossed the porch the one time before, ten minutes ago, and inside told the woman that I'd unfortunately run into the neighbors and she said, "And you would have to come in here." She was immediately busy with two children on an articulation table of some sort, I thought at first an abdominal-exercise machine, and I suppose by one argument it was but it was finally more technical than that. And the older child on one end of the table that I took to have Down syndrome got up and crawled onto the smaller child at the other end of the table and affected to smother it with a lawn chair, to everyone's delight, and I noticed through a window back toward the porch two girls exercising in wheelchairs, pulling themselves therapeutically up and down the room, one of these girls apparently disfigured or mutilated and covered up and the other absolutely striking but paralyzed in the legs, and ho, this was a bit of a rough scene here all of a sudden, where ten minutes ago this woman had just offered herself without all these complications, just these perfect rouge silver-dollar areolae in an open shirt, which is why I had gone down to the pond and washed up and jogged back, and found all this. Man. Locating succor is getting hard.

Longing

The kind of exhaustion I am talking about is, simply, or not simply, the broken heart. It makes you long to hold hands with someone you have not hurt who has not hurt you. This longing would be immediately and hotly extant if a dark girl offered you a cup of flan.

Dizzy

The aerie feather-brained quality is upon me today, I am slightly dizzy and nauseated. Got to ride over to the foundry and smelt some ore. My eyeglasses are featuring that snot-smeared effect. I hate that. My buddy was chased by a pack of dogs that scared him so bad he shat a little in his pants, and he hates that. I knew several distinguished older men who have died who had a better grip on things than I do. I wonder if they can see me floundering. I know that one of them in particular, with a scotch and pretty women about him in heaven, would enjoy sending annoying telegrams of advice like "Buck up" if he could. Most of them, though, I suppose would elect not to send a telegram even if they could. This is why they were regarded as distinguished on earth. They had the astute capacity not to deign, presume, meddle. They hunkered down within the castle walls of their particular potency, whatever it was, and did not send loose emissary of themselves about the uncharted ground of their purlieu.

It seems to me that if you do not deign, presume, and meddle, though, that the forces of the world at large, sometimes in the form of a kind of anonymous aggregate power, will pile up on you in an ambient deigning and presuming and meddling that will render you helpless. It is this way today: I am helpless here, dizzy and looking through badly fouled glasses at the bright, challenging world. Of course a non-anonymous, specific, particular force can deign, presume, and meddle with you also, like the phone company, or Ms. Trujillo at the phone company, who might withal be said to be but an accidental agent of aggregate force. But if, say—oh, you get the picture, you must, you are in the picture yourself. If you don't get the picture and fancy yourself not in it, I would say you are deigning to presume and are meddling with me, tacitly accusing me of being off rocker a bit. You are part of the problem. But I do not think that you are part of the problem. I think you are with me. I think you and I could dance across this floor of doubt in a cuddly promenade if we could know what our feet are up to. If I knew what my feet were up to, I would be distinguished, alive or dead. It is easier to be distinguished dead than alive.

I have lost the capacity to make a fist with my head, is what I mean. It is a matter of mental muscle tone, and I've gone as slack as pudding. I need to drink me some brain Jell-O, get some pearls growing in that oyster. At the very least I've got to wash my glasses and shut up.

Dusk

At dusk, the girls visit. We ride out to meet them on our horses, with our guitars. Our guitars are made of boxwood.

The girls are of flesh and they are agreeable to our every suggestion profane and genteel. They come at dusk. By dawn they are gone wherever they go. We live in a valley of cattle and history. Conditions are dry but there is water in the wells. All in all it is Spanishey.

The boxwood is a small hedge in my experience, and that my guitar is made of boxwood troubles me. The girls are taken with the tunes from our guitars, withal.

In history there has been force and badness and an eking along of goodness. There are broken guitars, but also new guitars. The girls are broken, but whole and trying. We too. We meet them when they come at dusk, at the gates of the ranch, a good place to meet. The cattle, the air, the past, etc. is there to enrich the moment. We are there with our boxwood guitars. The girls smile every night. They smile just the same way.

We will not be able to hold this moment forever, though we will try rabidly. A rogue boxwood plant on the impossibly long drive to the gate to meet the girls holds us in thin regard.

In history, before this moment and after this moment, some powerful men will drive this impossibly long drive with Mercedeses and it will be possible, the drive. The girls they meet will not be coming to them on foot, however, and will not be smiling. In a Mercedes, in fact, the drive will look practical. There will be no guitars, not of boxwood or anything else, then. Their girls will not be wearing colorful handmade skirts as ours do. The skirts are so folksy and authentic you couldn't take it if they were not on genuine girls who have come to see you. The men of Mercedes history, before this and after this, will have to drive far to procure their women, and the women will wear basic black and be expensive. That kind of woman is not for us, indubitably not for us.

Our names are so common we have forgotten to use them for some time. It has not mattered. We probably have not actually forgotten what they are, our names, but it might be close. We would abjure a test. We remember our girls at dusk and our guitars. I remember the boxwood holding me in its shrinking regard. How is there enough wood in the plant of a boxwood, or in many of them, to make a guitar? Does my guitar speak to the plant? Does the plant weep, or mourn, to see us pass with our guitars of itself? If you think this way, you are compelled to drive the impossible drive on a horse, not in a Mercedes. The horse has some non-Mercedes thoughts of its own. The girls are not about to be seen getting into Mercedeses either. We have all gone the other way. We are not powerful, except in our disregard for power, which is a weak form of powerfulness, we are not under delusions here. We are clear-headed, clear-voiced, clear-intended to our girls, who come at dusk.

Their skirts are a sunset under their smiles, and a sunset is behind their smiles, the same every night. Our guitars speak to the girls, to history, to the boxwood who disapproves of us. We inhale the history in the air, the past, present, and future. Too much of that will give you a headache so we do not do too much of that. Too much of that will accelerate your forgetting your name also. One girl is named Angelique. One is browner than the others and looks chewier, if to say that would not give offense. We deem, now that we have said it, that it would, so we retract it. Shall we say that the browner girl appears sturdier than the lighter girls, that her smile in the dusk appears brighter because her white teeth flash in greater contrast to her face than the teeth of the lighter girls flash, etc., and so the possibly very fraudulent conclusion may be drawn that the browner girl is happier and therefore readier for the rough handling that men with boxwood guitars and no car are going to mete out? And that these men who regard men in Mercedeses as *caciques* in history, even if they are but heavily mortgaged realtors, are the kind who would formulate that a girl looks chewier not with an eye to offending but merely with an eye to avoiding blather? Yes. She looks chewier then. Very chewy and she gives us a good feeling just being around her, as do equally the other girls, the less chewy-looking ones in the dusk. They are every bit as chewy-looking in the full day and in the full night. The browner girl has this advantage only for a few minutes per day. That does not seem unfair.

The guitar is easy to tune, the Mercedes not. As men of the weak powerful sort, who abjure the test of name recall, our own, we abjure also the notion of fairness, we know better, but it creeps into our thoughts sometimes, like bilge water. It obtains, pitch all you want. No craft does not leak. The thin boxwood holding us in thin regard was eaten by a bull. Or an antelope for all we know. We do know we had to run, guitars and girls bouncing a lovely discordant concerto across the present frame of history, from a shorthorn bull as wide as three Mercedeses and half as fast, but not for an impossibly long distance. The girls were happier and chewier all after that, our guitars sounded more splendid than usual, and all of us but me had failed to notice the missing boxwood.

Letter from France

I have, I think, two apartments in France and so seldom use one of them that I somewhat forget I have it or where it is when I do recall, alarmed, that I have it. In this respect it is like the course exam you are scheduled to take in dreams for a course you have not attended and do not comprehend your enrollment in. My second apartment, or first if you will, is somewhat more on the map of consciousness—to say, I have a clearer idea of what it looks like and where it is (it is airy and on the front of a building; the other is dark and in the high dank rear of a building)—and I believe I have spent time in it, but not much. This must leave me actually living yet somewhere else. I am in general very nervous in France.

My brain and my heart are as small as a songbird's. I tweet a little, flit, do not overthink. My emotions are a green and purple sorbet.

I wear a corset and a codpiece under my clothes. Whenever I am tempted to act, rare, I step back and secretly tighten the undergarments to further restrict motion, and thereby the temptation to act. A life of action is a wasted life.

Julie-New Sanchez-Manchez-Holt-Durgen is coming over for some covert sex that I may not appear to be very interested in lest it put her off that I am a typical male. The fact is that I am not up for appearing uninterested in sex, whether that is typical male or not, and I am not up for the sex with Julie-New Sanchez-Manchez-Holt-Durgen itself, whether that is typical male or not. I am not altogether up for a visit by Julie-New Sanchez-Manchez-Holt-Durgen except insofar as she can give me some inadvertent clues about my apartments. Sometimes I think I am living in her apartment and she is coming not to visit me but to discover me in her place, at which point she might legitimately expect to govern how I act with respect to sex or anything else. I wish I could get some claritude on some of these issues. The weather outside has shifted from a pleasant balm to some kind of typhoon-acting thing that has the walls heaving in and out visibly, audibly straining. I have wedged a towel into the front-door sill to stop the seepage of water. I have activated a small electric teakettle and I plan to drink tea if I find some. I will hold a warm crockery cup in my hands and take comfort in the warmth. The tea would soothe my nerves were my nerves unsoothed. My nerves are soothed in direct proportion to the force of wind around them. I feel as calm and serene as a dead man.

I read that Ted Turner has lost all his money and that there is some talk, commingled with the historical end of his father, of Ted Turner's killing himself. I pray that this is not the direction Turner rides his sunset pony toward, and in fact now that the little teakettle is starting to whistle I say, and I say it out loud, in the apartment I think in France that I myself rent or do not, Ted, do not ride your sunset pony that dark way. Steer the mean little bastard into the light, Ted, and don't let it bite you. You have a million dollars in your pocket and Kofi will just have to wait on the billion, so you keep on keepin' on, Ted. If I can, you can.

Wearing a Meat Shirt and
Killing a Snake

Taupist cold-cut shirt. We were wearing that. Them. A shirt of cold-cut discs, like shingles or chain-mail medallions. They were fragrant, the discs, the shirt. We were nervous, not knowing if large animals would attack us. We hoped that olive loaf would appeal even less to them than it did us. The Taupists make these shirts, we presume. We further presume they are some kind of monks, meat-shirt-making monks. The Taupist label in the shirt said Do Not Remove Under Penalty of Flogging, or We Will Make You Wear This Shirt a Long Time in the Sun. We could see ourselves in the sun in the meat shirt drying up like fish scales and being pink and rancid and then green and rancid and we were afraid to tamper with the Taupist label or to take the shirt off.

I broke into an apartment seeking information on snake hunting in the area and discovered three loose rattlesnakes in the apartment. One of them crawled near my brother whom I told to be still, but he was agitated and the snake bit him in the shoulder blade and hung on. I ripped it loose and slammed it on the floor, uncharacteristically. I was having trouble with 911 when the girl whose apartment it was let herself in, and I told her who I was and apologized for killing one of her snakes and said I was having trouble with 911. My brother was by this time in the bathtub to his jawline in hot water, giggling. Outside the bathroom the girl had taken off her shirt and bra and was on the floor in her skirt looking attractive (very brown and firm); she waved me away when I veered toward her. In the other room I found her brothers in karate gis. They attacked me with a lot of Oriental postures. I could not persuade them not to try to defend the honor of their sister, or of their sister's apartment, or snake, or whatever it was they were defending. I could not control them, or their sister, or 911, or my brother. All I could control was the snakes, and I had stupidly killed one of them. Had I thought about it I'd have said it was not a good day overall.

And when we finally worked up the courage to take off the meat shirt and drop it in the desert, where it sent a spiral of delicious toxicity up into the nostrils of buzzards, and we were certain that Taupists, whoever or whatever they were, were not in pursuit of us, we felt like having ice cream. You would, in the desert, having shed your meat shirt, understandably want some ice cream, born of cream and sugar and ice and salt, and of course you can walk, or ride, a long way in the desert, whether in a meat shirt or not, afraid of Taupists or not, with a belief that such a thing as a Taupist who would manufacture a meat shirt and require you to wear it under penalty of flogging exists or not, before you find ice cream.

You can in fact walk a long time in the desert having shed your Taupist cold-cut-disc shirt, or still wearing it, hoping for ice cream and knowing, in equal measure, there will be no ice cream. Your walking and hoping, and knowing and despairing, will not abate. You will be an honest and clear-headed and perplexed and dishonest man, or woman, all at once. You will be like unto a dog. This, this steady trudge of belief and disbelief, is what you were made for. If you have shed your meat shirt and happen upon another meat shirt you might, and probably will, put it on and carry it on your voyage until you shed it, and then find another, and don it, and shed and don and shed and don all the livelong day. You will be approaching the end and denying it is the end. One step is knowing, the next step not knowing, one caring, one not, one presuming, one not, one believing and the next disbelieving and the next believing and the next disbelieving. This tiny pendulum is the engine of your heart, the motor of man. You will litter money and feces along the way. Kill and maim fellows and flora and fauna, and pollute. Wear meat shirts again and again. Be afraid of Taupists, then discredit Taupists. Debate the existence and nature of Taupists. And, finally, expire, to the relief of all.

We are glad to be rid of you, despite our maunderings at the cemetery, and we will be glad to join you, despite our hand-wringing and heel-digging. We'll be there with you in the end, happy and done ourselves with the bipolar daily marching lies.

Spy

My daughter has become a spy. One prepares for surprises, but still. I had braced most against tattoo and mutilation, particularly the multiple perforation of the ear giving it the aspect of a python's lip, and metal deep on the tongue also is very high on the low list of things I wanted to see, so her working for the CIA, if that's who it is, has thrown me. She did not talk to me before her employ, and now she has official authorization not to talk to me. Trying to find out where she has been on a Saturday night may be a breach of national security. Instead of the hand, which I used to get, as she walked away from me, now I get a patronizing look as she holds her ground: Dad, the look says, please, I was on a date with Uncle Sam, *okayee*? She does not retreat into the cover of her room, but pours a bowl of cereal and begins to eat it, open-mouthed, a secret agent staring me, nosy security risk, down.

As a young man I protested CIA recruiting on campus and clearly failed. They got her on a high-school campus, apparently, where we never would have suspected they'd go. I have come to the horrible suspicion that I am directly responsible for her taking up with the CIA by buying her as I did last year a BMW. Can the CIA have a spy in suburban American without wheels? Without good wheels? I bought her the good car so that she would not be broken down on the side of the road, and apparently the CIA thinks the same way. This at any rate is one straw I grasp at. One may grasp at straws all day. As my fuddiness comes on, accelerated by having a daughter not out of high school working in government intelligence, it would be appropriate for me to be code-named Straw Grasper were I to get in the field. My daughter wears a wire, I a diaper.

Now the spy wants a better sound system in her BMW. You would think that a matter precisely up her employer's alley, not mine. "Why can't they add a CD changer and a do a speaker upgrade when they install the transponder?" I ask her. She looks at me with a patronizing smile, slightly shaking her head in that universal gesture of condescending incredulity.

You are so sad, this little one-millimeter shake of the head says. "Who is *they*, Dad?"

"The transponder people," I say. I don't say "The Agency" because I know better. "The Man. Let The Man buy some high fidelity."

The proposition seems to be that a girl in her BMW without a subwoofer lifting bark off trees does not look like a proper girl in a BMW but suspiciously quiet, like a spy. My daughter the secret agent cannot of course articulate this to me; she merely says her radio rattles at high volume, that, in fact, "My radio sucks if I turn it up." It sucks.

It has not snowed here in thirty years, and today it is snowing.

Thang Phong and the Son
of the Chief of Police

I wake up stunned and hurt. Should I not do sit-ups and push-ups until this little fit of stunned and hurt passes over?

The son of the ex-chief of police, gone to seed, walks fatly and loosely down the street.

Thang Phong (*tong pong*) will murder his piano teacher, whom he loves, or loved, very much, and respects, and calls, or called for years anyway, and probably will not stop calling after he has killed her, a "word-crass piano prayer." Thang Phong will not be able to say why he killed her. He will remain cheerful about his long and successful tutelage under her and is himself accomplished at the piano, for which he gives all credit to Mrs. . . . We have, strangely, misplaced the name of the piano teacher—precisely, we have forgotten it. It is like Harrison or Garrison but slightly off, perhaps in a French or German way.

•

It is a little sloppy to say that the son of the police chief has gone to seed. The son of the police chief was not ever in that state one is in before he goes to seed—would it be ripe? In full bloom? At stud? Is a horse put to stud after his racing career not "gone to seed"? The son of the police chief was not ever virile or prepossessing or upstanding, but he was a young man with a nice fresh face and possessed of a cheer, if not an innocence, that you did not expect of a boy whose father was locally famous for enmeshing himself in minor scandal and being, after all, the chief of police. By one argument the sons of police chiefs are *born* gone to seed. There is no hope for them: they are juvenile delinquents whose fathers will keep them out of the system of juvenile jurisprudence. But this particular boy showed hope of a sort. He was, well, *nice*. It is easy to say now, having seen him before, and seeing him now, *perhaps too nice*. Something went awry. Like milk in a bottle, something spoiled. The teeth in the nice smile of the bright child of the police chief are now furry-looking, and there is too much saliva in the smile, which he still proffers. He is soft-looking now, and weak-looking, and a bit splay-footed. He has as he walks no apparent direction. That is not quite accurate. He has direction, but not enough speed to suggest he is really going anywhere he needs to go; nor is he ambling in such a carefree way that he appears to be walking for health. It is impossible to say what he is up to. He is the fat son of the police chief who, the son, was once almost handsome now with dirty teeth and an oblique smile and a loose walk. He looks like a young man who has said to himself, "I have nothing better to do, I should at least walk somewhere," and has obeyed his own command. His father lost his office finally by claiming falsely to have played football for a famous football coach. He had also dislocated the affections of voters by wearing makeup for televised press conferences. This was not the casual makeup applied last-minute by a television crew to prevent a subject's nose from shining, but makeup that the chief of police self-administered in unartful excessive quantity toward an apparent attempt to have himself resemble Elvis Presley. People seeing the chief of police in this plumage did not think of Elvis so much as they thought of men who liked to dress up as women. The son of the ex-chief of police ambling about as he does looks lost.

Had an observer seen the initial contact between Thang Phong and the son of the chief of police, he would have said it appeared to be accidental and he would be baffled by its escalation and its outcome. The first shambling misstep a little across the sidewalk by the son of the chief of police into the path of the approaching Phong, Phong's halt, their both sidestepping the same way back over to the son of the police chief's initial side of the sidewalk, their both stepping then back to Phong's side, was a classic Willie Pep maneuver in which both parties, seeking to allow the other pass, inadvertently block the passage of the other. Perhaps it was the smiling, the wet yellow grin, by the police chief's son, which smile does not seem to be extinguishable, a fact Phong could not have known—perhaps this salacious-looking expression on the face of the fat boy in his way put Phong on the defensive, made him think a large grub-like Westerner was deliberately fucking with him.

Unlike the police chief's son, Thang Phong had direction and conviction: he was, before this clown got in his way, on stride and on time, precisely on time, for his piano lesson with Mrs. Guerre or Mrs. Garre or Mrs. Huarre. In his head he was going over the piece he was to play for her when suddenly someone was blocking his way and apparently finding it funny, and to Phong's acute sense of smell the boy seemed unwashed. This sour-milk smell might have panicked Phong, for he was antiseptic in his outlook and habits. He touched the son of the police chief deftly in the solar plexus with his middle finger and the son of the police chief collapsed on him. The finger went to the correct spot and stiffened from Thang Phong's root, which came out of the ground with the power of the earth. It was a thing Thang Phong had not thought of since a boy when they had all done martial arts as, say, American boys all do Little League baseball. He knew how to touch the son of the police of chief with maximum effect, and without malice, just as an American man will know, thirty years later on a softball team, to charge a grounder, when he would otherwise wait for the ball to come to him. When Thang Phong's middle finger went into the soft center of the police chief's son, with his two other fingers flanking it in what he had known thirty years ago was called a snake strike, he touched something down in there very firmly, like playing that gratifying E-flat in the opening of Beethoven's fifth, and the boy shuddered as the piano would, but unlike the piano the son of the chief of police lost his breath and grasped for Phong to try to keep from going down to the sidewalk. The clabbery smell and the clammy feel of the son of the chief of police panicked Phong more deeply as he was grabbed onto, and he twisted hard and inadvertently elbowed the boy in the temple, again with a ground-root force that he did not intend and that seemed to come from the provinces of both martial arts and music. The police chief's son's creepy smile dimmed a bit and he went to the side and down hard on the sidewalk, hitting first on blubber and then on his head, and he did not move.

Thang Phong was upset that this encounter had made him late for his lesson with Mrs. Legare. It did not occur to him that the man in his way was hurt. He wanted now to somehow take a shower before playing his piece for Mrs. Garreisen but he knew this was impractical short of his getting there and asking her if he could take a shower. You did not do that at a piano lesson or at any other occasion when entering someone's home, and especially in Mrs. Heinson's house it would be a problem because she would have to set out a matching set of towel and face towel and washcloth for him and these would have to match the rugs in the bathroom, which matched covers on the tank of the toilet and the cover of the toilet, which upholstery Thang Phong had already made note of in his innocent use of the bathroom on other less trying occasions when he had merely needed a toilet and not a shower. He resolved to march through the pain of being dirty and play his piece well for Mrs. Garhoolie and not be such a whiner.

But when he got there, a tad breathless from hurrying, and Mrs. Jeemstripe opened the door and received him with her warm smile as she did every week, he burst out, "Mrs. Hometapes, some crodhopper slime me, I needa take shower prease." He was wrong to have anticipated an ordeal, because even though, as he had predicted, a complete matching stack of high-grade earthtone terrycloth was supplied him, it was done instantly, without fuss, and Mrs. Thorsenguille even drew the water and had the shower running and was closing him into the bathroom before he could say another word and retract his request and insist he could play with germs on him almost as well as he could play without germs on him. The image of Mrs. Tomarre smiling at him so solicitously as she closed the bathroom door was so motherly and generous and she seemed so genuinely happy in being helpful this way that he thought of her at that moment as his mother, and he could not momentarily picture his own mother. He said aloud, "Who was my mother?" No image or idea of his mother or of any family at all came into his head, which he held in one hand, trying to think, absently fondling his genitals in the shower stream with the other hand, when the shower curtain ripped open and Mrs. Theneglassen stood there naked and white as a powder puff except for her dark triangular business in the middle of the largest white triangle of her, grinning at him hugely, stepping in, and Thang Phong recoiled and slipped and going down he grabbed behind him for purchase with the hand that had held his head while he had tried to think, and with the hand that had absently been at his genitals he formed and sent the snake strike that was now becoming second nature to him into Mrs. Horbeglieve's throat.

My problems exceed those of Thang Phong. But not by much. I am freshly divorced and at the age (a preserved fifty-plus) that forces young women to gauge their readiness to take on a man as old as their fathers, with a fathery set of smells. The less imaginative of them, which is nearly all of them, regard a fifty-year-old man's owning a red sports car a midlife crisis, a phrase of which they are most fond. The intractability of young women is not my real problem; it is but the problem I like to think about. The real problem is that I have no ambition or desire for anything at all—not for the women, not for work, not for barbecuing, not for life. If I have a problem, it is that I have no problem.

I have made Thang Phong also have, strangely, no problem where he should have a huge problem. He reached toward Mrs. Wallenstein more for balance than to strike her, which he did only inadvertently, as was the formation of the snake strike inadvertent (for the second time in the day, for the second time in thirty years). He dressed neatly, refolding the towel he lightly used, and left Mrs. Thorsen where she lay asphyxiated on the mauve polyester bath mat that also matched the toilet upholstery and the towels. He was remorseful to see her indisposed like that but not overcome by grief or anxiety. Two people had tried to put germs on him within a space of about twenty minutes and both of them had fallen down. Mrs. Terrebone had been *really* going to put some germs on him.

Mrs. Treglassen was found the following week, assumed to have slipped and crushed her trachea on the edge of the tub, which she had in fact done after Phong touched her, and no inquiry was made. The son of the chief of police was found by the coroner to have died from a heart attack with an incidental non-fatal blow to the head from his fall, which was accurate. No witness saw Thang Phong at either site and no one thought to inquire of him if he had had his lesson with Mrs. James on Friday and been thereby possibly the last person to see her alive. He would have said he had a very instructive lesson and that he had indeed been the last person to see her alive if they said so.

There are secret thoughts that each of these people had during these somewhat sad, possibly tawdry, conceivably whimsical events I have recorded. The son of the chief of police, as he Willie Pepped with Thang Phong and could not get by him, suddenly thought that if his father had said he played for Barry Switzer instead of Bear Bryant he would still be in office—it was dumb to lie but there were smart lies and stupid lies—and then he just could not breathe and tried to grab the guy in front of him to keep from going down. Mrs. Horve thought she should have taken Thang's hand at the keyboard during any one of their hundreds of piano lessons instead of going whole-hog overboard like this and probably scaring the poor thing to death, and then she too just could not breathe. When she saw Thang Phong falling backwards with an alarmed expression on his face, she felt a small hurt of rejection for just a second before the more pressing issue of *no air* overrode her hurt feelings and in fact wiped her emotional slate, which had been moments ago bristling with hope and energy and girlish moist ideas, clean.

With the police chief's son tackling him as it were, and smelling awful, and as hot and moist as dim sum, Thang Phong thought,

Why you even *in* my country, get *off* me (the violent elbowing twist that sent the boy to the ground came with the word *off*). When Mrs. Grieveport slashed open the curtain and he saw all her puffy whiteness, he was still desperately trying and failing to conjure an image of his own dark mother. His reaching back and forward to prevent falling had no thoughts within it; one merely never wishes to fall, especially on porcelain. The urge to not fall on porcelain is pre-intellectual.

Thang Phong did not ever realize that he was connected to the death of the son of the chief of police, because he never read in the paper about the boy's being found dead of a heart attack on the sidewalk, and he did not know about the police chief's troubles, or his troubled boy, or any of it. About Mrs. Nielson's demise he knew he was responsible, but in a defensible if regrettable manslaughtery self-defensive accidental way only. The guilt that was natural he sought to assuage by playing the piano intensely at concerts that in any way memorialized her: at recitals of her former students, say. When he played at venues unrelated to her, he often found a way to mention that she had been his best teacher and that he considered her not only a world-class teacher but a world-class player in her own right.

It gives me some pleasure, at a time when I have come to not take pleasure in pleasure, to hazard that Thang Phong loved Mrs. Jones, and loves her still. In time of course he came to recall his own mother clearly, but the image of his naked piano teacher reaching for him still comes much more readily to his mind.

Breakdown

One does not decide to stop being oneself; one merely stops deciding to be oneself. There is a quotient of energy the expenditure of which is necessary for one to be perceived in a way one is accustomed to, and to perceive oneself in a way one is accustomed to. And this expenditure becomes optional, its expense even a matter to chuckle at. It is like the energy required to eat meat and to be perceived as a red-blooded kind of dude. Suddenly, or gradually, it would be just as well to be a vegetarian, or anything else. The energy for holding course is gone. It is the incipience, this waving away of the compass bearing, of a nervous breakdown, a term that would disturb someone still holding course but a prospect that sounds inviting to someone waving off the compass. So, ladies, what I mean to say is that I have become a vegan in my head and no longer care who I am or who you think I am. I realize all this makes not a large ripple on the universal pond of vanity.

A bear skinned-out resembles a man, I have heard. This apparently disturbs hunters who have not been disturbed to that point in the adventure of killing a bear. But they get the willies once the hide sits there and the naked bear here.

Mrs. Stamp

A little dialogue played one morning in Mrs. Terrell Stamp's head:

Don't sit on that knife.

I can sit on these knives?

Yes. Sit on those, but not on that one there.

These here are okay?

Yes. Sit right on them.

Like this?

Yes. You can squirm down on them, they won't hurt you.

Are they rubber?

No, they are not *rubber*. God. They are just . . . well, sittable knives, and that one is not a sittable knife.

Mrs. Terrell Stamp had many things on her mind, but foremost was marble cake in the morning. It was cold outside and she was happy to have her ingredients inside. She might go outside but if she did it would not be because she had to but because she wanted to. She liked to let good cold air come up her skirt for just a shot, then head back to the oven she could stand near while making the cake. She specialized in marble cake because she liked the wide tolerances involved in folding in the marbling fudge cake. There was not a right way or a wrong way to fold. If what was in one bowl got into what was in the other bowl, you had succeeded, more or less. You could do it without taking your eyes off a soap opera. There was precision cooking, and certainly other precision adventures in life, and Mrs. Terrell Stamp sought to avoid them. She liked loose, relaxed things, like popping out into the snow in a skirt for a minute, making a cake while looking at TV, leaning against the stove and thinking about nothing but how nice the stove was after the snow, how good the cake was beginning to smell, how crummy the soaps were but you kept watching largely because they were crummy. That was their point: loose art for the loose. You could have a marble cake that was not pretty, just as you could have, say, a dalmatian with heavy unattractive spots, but you liked the dog anyway, and you liked the cake too. That's how she liked life—heavy or clumsy or inelegant or not smart, but good anyway.

When the children got home from school in the afternoon she remembered who they were and how many they were and loved them. Raising children was the loosest, most imprecise art of the widest conceivable tolerances, to her mind, of any enterprise on earth, except perhaps drug addiction of the terminal sort. Half of daily television was now devoted to the premise that already loose parents should not attempt to raise children. She'd seen a sixty-year-old mother in a bikini try to mount a talk-show host in front of her own daughter. This had of course been an attempt to tighten up the daughter. The mother was screwed up, of course, but she was not incognizant of the underlying principles at work: appear tight, stay loose. The mother had hit on the errant proposition of appearing loose as well, an experiment that was failing. The daughter was aghast at the mother though, so it was debatable really whether the experiment would fail. It was unlikely, at any rate, that the daughter was going to try to mount the host after the mother had pawed him. And she would now in all likelihood hesitate before wearing an immodest bathing suit. Perhaps the crazed mother was genius. She was a bag of frenetic cellulite with badly dyed hair. Mrs. Stamp could not see her maintaining course too much longer.

The show made her nervous, as they all did: an entire industry predicated on, and capitalizing on, the fact that Americans did not know how to properly have children or to eat. The soap operas tried to demonstrate the opposite fiction: that we were infinitely sexy and slim and in and out of love in mysterious and glamorous continuum. Television offered a dramatic commercialized equivalent to her little polar minuet between the cold snow and the warm stove.

In a contemplative *penseroso* of this sort one morning in her kitchen, the roof of her entire house lifted off, almost noiselessly, and spun away, up up and away as if in a cartoon. It was non-threatening, this putative tragedy, so that Mrs. Stamp had occasion to be reminded of Dorothy's house spinning as it left (or returned to?) Kansas, for her roof spun also, that slow, screwing spin that things approaching or leaving earth do, having something, she thought, to do with the earth's spinning beneath them. Her roof sucked off the house like a tin of coffee being opened and spiraled off, dropping on her a small gentle rain of pink insulation tufts like mimosa blossoms. A sprinkling of roofing nails tinkled easily onto the kitchen floor. She could suddenly see how filthy her kitchen was, far more disturbing than the roof's leaving. The weather outside was pleasant; what she could see of it, brushing insulation from her face, was what they meant when they said partly cloudy. There was no wind, no darkness to account for the roof's spinning away to Oz or to outer space or to the nearest trailer park or strip mall. It would be a fine irony, and a sure sign of the hand of God, if the roof landed in a trailer park and did damage. Over the years He had hurled all the trailers he could and He was now ripping up parts of better built homes and throwing them at the trailers. Mrs. Stamp checked out her kitchen and it was all in working order. She still had water, gas, and the television was still on in the next room. What a pleasant day it was. The phone worked too. She should call someone and report the roof but did not know whom to call. She hated decisions and she most hated decisions involving telephones.

There was no immediate problem with the roof beyond cleaning her kitchen and, she supposed, the entire house, now that it lay exposed to the light of day. Maybe she should call a cleaning service. That made some sense, but so did calling a lawyer and divorcing her husband, and so did calling a travel agent and booking a flight to Alaska, where as a young woman she had always wanted to go, but the importance of having a roof over her head had stopped that and other nomadic impulses. She had heard of families living in tents during the Depression and wondered if the tenability of that were soon to be demonstrated to her. Rather than walk outside, she climbed up on the kitchen counter and looked out of her house to see if other houses had suffered roof loss. They all appeared to be intact, and no one was out there gawking at hers. This was the first moment in which she wondered if her mental state might be not in order. Was her head really extending over the open wall of her kitchen peering at the unharmed houses up and down and across the street from hers, or was it somewhere else? Had it, her head, spun to Mars, leaving her house intact? Would a phone call prove the matter?

She decided it would not. Even if she called a cleaning service and they sent a crew of alcoholics who hauled her carpets into the yard and steamed her entire house and blew it spic and span with an industrial compressor—she imagined this with real pleasure— and they chatted about the remarkable missing roof and what a boon to true cleaning it was, she and the sots about ready for her to break out the beer in reward for their Herculean ordeal, there would be no knowing that the entire affair was not delusional.

What could she do? She had no idea, and usually having no idea what to do was a good inspiration for her doing nothing, but it felt different in this case. Sitting there in a roofless house did not speak of a sound mind. She'd look less suspicious somehow were she to bellydance from room to room in a roofless house, she thought. Yet it was also time to acknowledge that she was done calculating what was suspicious and how she would be perceived by others in what she did in life. This missing roof had put a foot down with respect to all that. She was clearly now on her own true, or false, path. She turned the TV off. Watching fat actual fornicators all day on the one hand and slender fake fornicators on the other had been fun, but it was over. The British call cookies "biscuits," she thought, and we call cookies "cookies" and biscuits "biscuits." She was going to be plain and correct from now on.

Bedtime

We did not know what to expect. The salamanders were cooking their own meals, having repudiated fast food with a viciousness that was surprising coming out of those soft-bodied gentle souls. They wore little chef hats and deftly used their tiny utensils and did not complain much as they burned themselves, which, given the deliquescent quality of their moist skin and the heat of the stove, was nearly constantly. In fact it looked as if what they were cooking most was themselves. The happy suffering of the salamanders in the kitchen put us into a nervous and humble and vaguely guilty state. They had devised a way of cutting a standard Band-Aid into 128 pieces for dressing their wounds. The kitchen smelled of these fresh Band-Aids and earthworms and of the odd things they cooked.

Well, by that I mean, since you ask, pancakes the size of Rockefeller dimes. Yes, you are right, not odd under the circumstances, given that they were pancakes for salamanders. Not odd at all. I have seen on a grown woman nipples the size of Rockefeller dimes, and that is odder than such a pancake fit for a salamander. To see those little dry pancakes going happily into those moist mouths was perhaps what I meant was odd. I have trouble meaning what I mean these days. I have trouble meaning anything at all. Am I not a grown man concerned with salamanders who cook, like cartoon characters? Can I actually *mean* this? To mean something you have to be capable of making a muscle with your brain, of bearing down mentally. I can no longer bear down. While this disturbs somewhat, it also does not disturb. If you can't bear down, nothing much bears down on you. If you are preoccupied with salamanders in the kitchen, it is as agreeable as being preoccupied by anything else, or by nothing at all.

We might as well forget the salamanders and their pancakes. We are free to move on to other concerns. I have none, but you perhaps have some. They would relate to the world, most probably—certainly they would relate to the world as opposed to the otherworld, a phrase that is attractive, as indeed we find the otherworld, whatever we mean by it, more attractive than the world. Why is this so, that we like a world that we can but feebly and variously only imagine exists over one in plain view before us? Is it not because the one before us is, in the parlance of the more eloquent of our children, messed up? We have so messed up the situation here that we prefer to think of an afterlife of beatitudes, or if we are not given to that sentimentality we select a finer one, a world not after but parallel and supernatural, usually peopled not by people but by weirdnesses made of goo and capable of thinking better than we do and fighting with more sophisticated weapons. Even the odd salamander who can cook will do. Why do we seek these other places full of alien forms? Is it because people are one big piece of shit? I verily submit that this is so. When you have reached this position, there is not a lot of what gets called wiggle room, and you don't feel like playing outside, or inside, anymore.

I have been traded back to my original team, which still does not want me. I play, and do not play, unwanted. It is not an enviable position, and I do not want to talk about it. I would rather talk about retardation, its onset and advance, considerable in my case, leading to my streamlighting into an ocean of ineptitude.

My testosterone has dried up. I never had courage, and now have not even bluster. This would be humiliating had I still balls. As it is, even humiliation is neutral. Some of you out there can understand this. Together we constitute a large human club but we are of course clubless. We do not require private rooms for our elite lounges. We sit on a bench here, stand on a corner there. We hardly remember our mothers and do not care. Or we do and we do care. There is no difference in what we do or do not do.

I am a goof guitar player, I believed in good shoes briefly but that belief too has succumbed to a risible and quaint erstwhile passionism, I will now go to bed. Lay me down to sleep, Jesus, you old bullyrag who first discovered these things I know.

The Flood Parade

I get back from the flood parade—a small flash flood is let through the streets to entertain the people—and discover my apartment filled with graduate students invited there by a colleague. They are watching television and he is testing a blowgun. I sit on a sofa next to a student. On the TV screen is a show featuring an actress I recognize as playing Miss Brooks from the show *Our Miss Brooks*; the actress appears to be the daughter of the woman who originally played Miss Brooks, Eve Arden. I inquire of the room if this is the daughter of Eve Arden and the students confirm it as if it is something everyone knows. They cannot possibly themselves know the show *Our Miss Brooks* or Eve Arden; their knowledge of popular culture is boundless if they know this to be Eve Arden's daughter without knowing Eve Arden. The woman next to me lets her hand fall to my collar and does not remove it. I touch her hand there and we engage hands; she plays with my ear and I play with her fingers. She leans over me to adjust the TV and I see her breast, about the size and contour of a Hershey's kiss. The party becomes very thick and this woman and I make a tour through it holding hands. We discover that we have flirted before and that I learned earlier that she is not available because she is involved with a young man some distance away who has threatened to kill himself if she leaves him. My position is that such an arrangement is unfortunate, and the woman agrees. A second woman at this point begins to vie for my affection in front of the first and I allow it to develop, watching the reaction of the first woman, whom I want badly. It is clear that she has taken her moral position with the welfare of suicides in mind. I drift around the party and discover I am in my underwear, not unlike the bulk of the partiers, but I nonetheless feel a little underdressed. I resolve to leave.

Getting You Some Cocktail

A cute girl with a nice pink backpack with a white cat in leaping silhouette on it has just gone by the window on a moped. I don't need her.

Last night a woman came and laid herself across both arms of the overstuffed chair I was in and asked if I did not want "some cocktail." I said I did not know what "some cocktail" could mean but that I guess I wanted some. I touched her stomach. She was on one elbow across the arms of the chair and her stomach was firm. I'll have cocktail if that's the thing to have, I said. I admired the tension of her stomach that I had touched but did not so comment. She knew that I admired the tension of her stomach but did not so comment. I teared up a bit. She touched the side of my face, paying attention at the same time to people behind the chair who might witness this. This woman was vaguely redheaded but not in that arsenical juicy weird true-redheaded way. She was bleached out by troubles of her own, but holding it together. She was going to engineer to get me some cocktail and see that I had a decent time. I was most thankful to her.

Solitude

We were so loaded that these loose bricks outside Bobby's place floated around in the house with us, directed by gentle commands like "Here, boy." They wanted to float into the refrigerator when you looked for beer in there and you had to shoo them out. We did not want to asphyxiate a brick in the refrigerator.

The meeting of the World Stone Club was called to order. Bobby started to read the agenda and the order broke down. Janey Farrington said all the girls were tired of taking off their shirts like it was the sixties and Julian said so what he was tired of his own name and wasn't going to do that anymore either. This was funny, not going to "do" his name, like a drug, so Phyllis took her shirt off and showed herself to Julian and Julian said he wasn't tired of that yet and he should not have been because in point of fact the shirts-off accord was best intended or designed or I should say, well I don't know what I should say except that it was Phyllis above all the girls, maybe really by that point she was the only girl, who had any business taking her shirt off, aesthetically speaking. She has ski slopes and puffies and it gave you a buzz.

I pushed a brick out of the way to see them clearly even though she had turned sort of privately to Julian, and the brick glided all the way out of the room into a lampshade in another room. Bobby's mother had died last week and the house was starting to show it. Nobody mentioned her. I had liked her though I never said anything to her. She wore these pastel dresses with belts and had a permanent in her hair. I don't know what she died of; she had not to my mind been sick and she was not old-looking either. It was in a small way like hearing June Cleaver or Harriet Nelson had died—you couldn't believe it but it probably happened. I was sitting there considering asking Bobby if he had buried his mother in the crawl space under the house like John Wayne Gacy when I looked over and Phyllis was on her knees against Julian on the sofa, grinding herself into his face, and Julian was crying and trying to suck on her, blubbering and slurping like the Sgt. Pepper's Lonely Hearts Club Band, a phrase I had never appreciated until that moment. He was a lonelyhearts and Phyllis had figured it out and she was giving him a tune to beat the band. It looked like a lot of fun. Her nipples were the color of the bricks, several of which were hovering near the action, like flies. Julian's eyes were the same color red from his crying. It honest to God looked like he was crying those bogus tears of joy you hear about. I was ready to cry a little myself. Crying a little is a good thing if you can turn it off.

This had never happened before, congress between members of the Stone Club during a meeting. The shirts-off thing had been political and we had been supposed to carry on like nudists. Now that the shirts-off thing had been repudiated, we were apparently free to act like reasonable people, so Phyllis mounted Julian and the rest of us watched and shooed bricks out of the way and wondered what Bobby had done to Mrs. Thames.

I got up and called a state park in Georgia I had been thinking about and booked a cabin for a whole week for $264. Some outright solitude would do me good. With outright solitude you can do nothing, just lie there and not get up, or get up and lie back down, all day, or all night or any other stupid misuse of time because there is no one to look over your shoulder, if that is the right expression, and that is another thing about solitude, no need to worry about the right or wrong expression because you needn't use any expressions at all.

I was just sitting there having put the phone down, thinking fondly of the prospect of my week in my cabin, which I knew was a good log cabin built in the thirties by the CCC except they had been fitted with new stoves and central air, when Janey Farrington slipped into the chair behind me and took the phone cord and got it around my neck and started to make like she was strangling me, and this was a trip because I think she was dwelling on Phyllis and Julian's thing and on Bobby and what he did to his mother too, plus being mock strangled was fun, and I turned to her and kissed her and she asked if she could go with me to the cabin without effing everything up, as if she had read my mind, because even if she heard the whole my side of the conversation with Georgia Parks or Reserve America dot com or whoever it was I didn't see how she knew what the cabin meant to me, maybe I had been talking out loud there. Anyway she was going *wrenk wrenk* with the cord, delivering these sound effects like the *Psycho* slashing scene a little, and these noises of exaggerated struggle like she was working hard to choke me out, and I got a brick-colored nipple in my mouth and started crying, and it felt really really really wonderful, I can't understand it, I can't understate it.

It was clear to me then that Bobby was going to have trouble getting anything done officially with the World Stone Club meeting. This somehow served him right, though to that point I had had no quarrel with Bobby at all. I got the phone away from Janey, who was now kissing me all "Love Me Tender" style, like she was in high school, and called 911 and said, "I am at the Robert Thames residence on Leesville Road, and we were told that Mrs. Thames died but we wonder if an investigation should not be made, no this is not an emergency, no I am not calling another number because I have called this one, thank you, good-bye." I returned Janey's kisses at that point. She said, "What did you do that for?" I said, "Because it feels good." She said, "No, call the police." I said, "I meant calling the police feels good but I see you thought I meant kissing you back feels good and it is too much work to straighten it out further and does it matter anyway, they both feel good," and we kissed some more without any more questions.

We were perfect idiots in a chair, happy. She tasted good to me, and I must have tasted good to her, as impossible as that sounds. The room was dim and I couldn't hear anyone else anywhere in the house and I did not see any bricks. Janey Farrington has irises that are very small and aquamarine. Her skin is fine and white. Her eyes look like some kind of seawater seen the wrong way through a telescope. It would not last for long, but it would last for a bit.

The Imperative Mood

Put that nice blue and white pitcher on the marble washstand. Determine your sock size. Play favorites. Have some. Be all you can be and all anyone else can be. Fall back and regroup. Be for heroes. Try not to fail. Recall your mother. Forget your father. Please release me. Let me love again. Trust that I will be okay.

Whatever floats your boat, go ahead and float it. Do not have large untenable quantities of despair. Do not go to parades. When you feed orphaned wild animals, do not expect them to make it. Be forewarned. Be careful that your genitals do not show outside the strict confines of your underwear. Learn at least three racquet games during your lifetime. Study the coin flip. Please understand, and have according sympathy when relevant, that pink-skinned people and animals have tender feet.

If I tell you that I have robbed a bank, prepare the correct reaction. Let us abort the mission, if we are on one. Supply me with the name of that comic who climbed into a condom and tell me if it was specially manufactured or off the shelf. Be more forgiving. Test the wind. Brave the currents. Be strong, strong, strong. Tell me my name. Be gone.

Go to harbor town and pee on someone's boat. Chase dreams. Smoke a pipe, or pipes. Fix the toilet. Put on those wax lips over there and wear them all day, I don't care how deformed and drooly they get, if you take them out at any point I will call the law. Try to keep your temperature in the accepted homeostatic range for humans, can you? Hand me that newspaper without letting it make a sound. If I make a sound reading it, be grateful that I, not you, made the newspaper make a sound. Just thank your lucky stars, young man, thank your lucky stars.

Sit in good old overstuffed chairs the livelong day and rejoice that you are not mixed up in the turmoil inside a church or outside the perimeter of a military position under attack or near an abortion clinic or in an airport. Prepare colorful drinks that are not particularly tasty but don't have to be—look at them! Call all your pets to you, living and more importantly dead. Keep your belt cinched just a tad tight. Believe in Jesus whether you do or not. Remove staples when you discover them not to be actually stapling things together and carefully discard them. Sing songs to ladies and appreciate the scarves they wear. Determine, were you to have put in your will the method by which you would like to be put to death, if this could have any bearing on how the state might put you to death should it come up.

Do not always be of good cheer; sometimes act as if you are a possum. Throw rocks at children. Leap tall buildings, of course. Remain calm. Try to win. Be winning whether you win or not. Declare bankruptcy not quite with pride. Alternate the theories you entertain about all things. Investigate leather tanning. Learn to swim again. Steadily decline in all your strengths until that steadiness is your strength. Purchase a packet of indigo dye and place it so that you can regard it every day. Call your friend who walked the wire in the circus and ask about the shoes. Change the linen. Realize yet again that for a long time you had too much courage to kill yourself or even entertain it but that now you can entertain it but have too little courage to do it. Regret that you have never seen a real cotton field in operation or a cotton exchange either and that these wants are both unrelated to many other things you should have witnessed but did not, both of the sort you can imagine and, worse, of the sort you cannot even conceive you are so small and deprived. Locate, purchase, and construct an industrial-grade galvanized swing set in your backyard, and if you do not have a backyard in the backyard of someone with a child whom you can convince that you mean the child no harm.

Try to be the best you can be, and the worst. Prepare for Armageddon. Get to the bottom of baking. Imagine a conversation with Charles Manson. Try things. Invent something. Dilute dilute dilute the Dr. Bronner's. Heap up the seconds. Take dance instruction, and step lively. Har' to lee. Ponder NASA photos and wonder if there isn't more wonder in them than you actually see. Run to the store.

Lecture the pets. Try all the doors and windows for fit and trim and of course security and attend anything found amiss. Give some thought to purchasing an incandescent lightbulb or two before they go extinct—would one in a very out-of-the-way place, seldom used, like the closet under the stairs, be so bad? Walk the yard looking for snakes without any thought of seeing one. Whistle for your dog dead now fifteen years. Clean the kitchen.

Pay a bill or two, get the phone, and reach out and touch someone. String the hammock and practice the diagonal lie. If this does not come naturally to you, reflect on just how far you are also from ever speaking Spanish naturally, or speaking it at all, or speaking any language at all, and admit that you are a retard uncomfortable even in a hammock who will need the Language Fairy to come down and put a language under your pillow if you are ever to have a foreign language. Envision some new, cool colors all through your house and go to bed.

List the wounds you do not want, in order: head wound, genital wound, ass wound, spleen wound, eye wound, extremity wound, thumb smash, skin scrape, splinter. Decide that you have had enough surgery and can go the rest of the distance unaided or propped up by the knife. Fill out that exhausting questionnaire and take it to the will attorney. Have a little buzz on when you go in there. Rule out radiation therapy along with the surgery. It's going to be the hammock and the perfected diagonal lie from here on in. Recall that frisky young whippersnapper Tennessee Williams whom you once so admired and still do. Recall that time you saw the 1% play for the first time. In your mind sit again on those pale green wooden stools in that cafeteria and watch Allen and Bob play in front of where the dirty thick-plastic beige dishes went in with the spaghetti sauce on them. Recite: Little Jack Horner sat in a corner, oh oh oh. Call North Carolina and see about a dog. Decide that deciding it is too late to rescue yourself may be itself rescue, but concede this salvation-by-surrender argument may be fallacious if not outright childish. Recall the boy in the back of the car saying, when someone in the front of the car derogated Elvis for liking the party girls to keep their panties on, "Just what's wrong with that!"

•

Hold your horses. Allow interest to compound, simply or whatever the other thing is. Do not have traffic today with a doctor. Read between the lines *only*; it's easier than reading the lines. In the event that armed men of any sort enter the building, watch their feet closely. Try to recall the smell of caged mice, and the image of the child of yours separating the twist ties one by one until they made a fine large mess that had to be put in a baggie, and the same child picking back up the flowers dropped in the aisle of her grandfather's wedding, and the same child telling you at age five, fishing, "Look, it goes under, and nothing! This is ruining my life."

Inspect the phrase "resistant incoherence" as it pertains to John Ashbery, whose incoherence you have not so much resisted as found incoherently beautiful. Realize that you cannot take time out like this for reveries so private when people are expecting you to get on with the business of telling them what to do. So, people: get yourselves on with the business of doing what you need to do, and realize that sometimes in every life that will necessarily involve wasting a lot of time on fruitless pursuit of that which can be interesting only to you, and only in a way that at some point you will invariably yourself declare the time to have been spent pointlessly—have at it! If Helen Vendler writes "resistant incoherence" and you want to roll that around in your mouth like an unsatisfying little candy trying to suck off the *-ant* and put in its place *-ed*, leaving you a more satisfying "resisted incoherence," because you resisted it, it is not resist*ant*, it is *incoherent*, well this is your business and your business alone and nobody's business *but*; yet even this improved candy is not that hot, what happened to the old horehounds that were so thrilling to pronounce as an adolescent, whore hounds!, whether they were actually good to eat or not, but they were, were they not? And were they not heavy heavy sassafras, not resistant sassafras but sassafras that you resisted because it was too strong, as like, well, sometimes people get too enthusiastic about how well they think they make dressing for turkey and overload it with sage? Recall the time Charlie Geer freehanded the grits into the pot of boiling water on Cumberland Island, the time his uncle woke up on the rolling waterbed with his exgirlfriendJoanieloveofhislife on the other side of it being boinked by the new guy. Don't ask people to go there. People, don't go there, just accept that Holmes Geer eventually killed himself, that I then taught his nephew in school after having gone to school myself with the uncle, and that the nephew taught me you can freehand grits, resistant instruction.

Put your nose close to the barrel of your shotgun right after you've shot a clay and get a good snifferoo of that smoke—delicious. Do not put your nose over the end of the barrel or you will be in violation of Safety Rule No. 1. Tell someone today of some event you fondly recall in your life and do not sentimentalize it, or do. Mourn the loss of your rooster, your Silver Duckwing bantam rooster that did not weigh one pound wet who fought you until he realized you were using the fights to catch and pet him. He was named Yeehi and it is perhaps prudent not to name birds if they are subject to slaughter by even the airhead neighbors' airhead dogs. Put up some signs that say No Dogs and let the airhead neighbors tell you they don't think their dogs, while certainly smart, can read.

Consider getting a lawyer so you can call him and ask him to survey your entire situation and discover if you are good for successful litigation against anyone and suggest that you do not want to die not having lived a full life and sued someone. Perhaps your will could be adjusted to offer him a bonus as executor if he has already by the time of your demise successfully prosecuted a lawsuit on your behalf, but mention that he is not to take this to mean that you are uninterested in a posthumous lawsuit on behalf of your estate. Take a big load of clothes to the Goodwill; take everything you own if you can stand to do it. Go to Walgreens on your way back and get a toothbrush and a vinyl ditty bag. Keep it minimal from here on in. Tap dance on pea gravel in the driveway. Do not lament the loss of testosterone. Do not whistle so that others may hear you. If you get an opportunity to facilitate someone's going to Alaska, seize it. If you can locate an old vacuum-tube clock radio, tune in a distant AM blues station if they still exist and listen to it at night with your hand on the warm plastic cabinet of the radio.

Try to recall the person you thought you were and the moment you began to realize you are not that person, and try to grasp and appreciate the high quality of lunacy required for you to have ever thought you were that person. Determine if it is reasonable to assume that there might be a conservation of sadness and happiness in the universe, as there is alleged to be a conservation of mass and energy. Ponder issuing a monograph called *The Thermodynamics and Quantum Mechanics of Human Emotion*, which will posit that the sloppitudes of human wants and fears and hopes and satisfactions and dissatisfactions and mournings and celebrations can be as precisely known as quantities of entropy and Gibbs free energy and the location of a particular subatomic particle, at a particular time, on the backside of the moon. Procure for yourself some good hard cooked cheese and eschew, as you do, raw soft cheese.

Prepare your backpack. Line up all the velcro closures in your environment. Pine Sol the entire joint. Skip down to the mailbox and disregard the mail when you get it home. Picture in the cumulus clouds above you on the mail run a dog it would not be bad to have with you on the ground. Ponder whether you really do have the balls to refuse medical treatments in the event you are diagnosed terminally or with something that might as well be. Call Mickey Milam and ask him if it is permissible for a person in this county to be put on a funeral pyre and burnt. Try to use up the can of sweetened condensed milk and resolve to never open another one. Try to figure out what thyme actually tastes like and how you could know oregano and cilantro but not tarragon and thyme. Don't regret anything today except the standard recycling regrets, and do not resist regretting those, which deepens and protracts the act of the regretting. Name Cloud Dog, if he would but come down, Nu-Ra Buddy in the Sky With Diamonds, and explain to him that he is sired by the most famous beagle in history out of a song by the Beatles, and say, "Beagle, Beatle—how cool is *that?*" to him, and watch him thump his tail in earnest gratitude for the attention and hold you altogether blameless for being an idiot. Resist the conclusion that if he does not perceive you to be an idiot he is an idiot himself. Show him a measure of the charity he shows you. Which is to say, love him with equal reciprocating indiscrimination and be for once, or for a few moments, which is what once means, a man as happy as a dog.

The infamous pit-dog-breeding drug-running money-laundering felon Lumbee Indian who called you recently and left a phone number he stumbled with and then called back and gave a corrected one for, neither of which works, so you cannot call him back now—call the Fayetteville Detective Bureau and leave a message that a friend of yours up there has you worried and maybe they know something, and when the silliness of this settles in on you after the call, look in the narcotics drawer and see what there is. Go downstairs and get the football with the split bladder beside your daughter's bed and take it outside and kick it into the woods. This will not be very far, since the thing holds no air, and after a day or so when the picture of mold on the dead football has a firm place in your mind go get the football and wipe it off well and put it back beside your daughter's bed. Say, out loud if you want to, pretending perhaps that the narcotics have taken effect and so you have excuse to talk to yourself, She is a handsome girl who will not die of loneliness and not a spindly boy (as I was) who would have died of loneliness (as I did), my prayers on this score were answered, and she has not lied to spindly boys and broken their hearts, my prayers ditto, so all in all I am feeling very good about her and about her liking footballs and I cannot kick this thing into the woods even if it were the case, which it is not, that its green deterioration there would not break my heart and keep me from sleeping and make me have to move.

Take yourself in hand. Get a heft of yourself, then prudently release yourself from hand: it is too late. Do not be overtroubled by the chicken's standing for you; you are her rooster and she must be herself. If you want to be troubled about something, be troubled that you let her rooster be killed by the airhead neighbors' airhead dogs unavenged. Today is a good day to give no one a hard time about anything, or today is a good day to give everyone a hard time about everything. You must decide how you wish to presume. Look up "salamander": you want the culinary meaning, which may well go back to medieval times. Do not oppress any of the women you have already oppressed, and try not to oppress any new ones. Try to get all the way to the grave, in fact, without oppressing another woman. You will need the equivalent of one of those harnesses that mechanically extracts the fainting lab worker from the immediacy of a noxious chemical reaction in research and manufacturing processes. Salute in your mind William "Mayo" Smith, who invented PVC using just such harnesses and who talks a good game of oppressing women but to your knowledge has not oppressed one yet, and yet he changed the world with his polyvinyl chloride. He in fact de-oppressed a lot of women, if we want to take a special-angle view of Mayo and his work, by reducing the time a woman might have to look at a plumber's butt crack to the time it takes a plumber to glue a PVC fitting together, about ten seconds. That is the speed of light compared to his threading and installing a piece of black pipe, and you should be in a position at all times to let the world know, and its women, what Mayo Smith has done for them. Just before you oppress another woman, you might, in fact, just say, Excuse me, I know Mayo Smith, and in his honor, lest it be besmirched by my staying here any longer, I have to go.

Admit the woman and her daughter to your house so that they can go to the ecology conference without staying at the Zen hostel. Have it explained that this is the eco conference, this month, not the solar-panel workshop, next month, for which you initially agreed to let them stay in your house, because a friend of yours asked if this was feasible and you said it was, not paying attention to dates, so when the woman called you naturally assumed she was on about the solar-panel workshop, but she was not, and now you have accepted the mother-daughter eco team twice into your house. Have it explained that the program of intense stretching and lymph-liberating mojo that she purports to trade for the room will take at least two and a half hours and that Sally, the daughter, was born here, and the only reason she was born at all is because Sheila Harr, a famous crazy landlord in the area, sixteen years ago during the Danny Rolling reign of terror, when she, the woman, demanded iron bars on the ground-floor windows because someone's boyfriend had merely crawled through a window to get to an upper room to get his shit back from the girl who'd kicked him out, and if an ordinary boyfriend just getting his shit could get in that easily what did it say about how easily Danny Rolling could cut all their heads off—on *day fifteen* Sheila Harr showed up with the iron bars, but she, the woman, was like, No I am already OUT of here, and went downtown to a large house with four men in it and took up with one of them, "And the rest is, well," she says, smiling and indicating Sally with a motion of her arm not unlike Vanna White's indicating a letter on the board, "history." Regard ever so slyly Sally standing there, who says, "That's great, Mom," and heads for the bedroom you have lent them. As soon as the mother goes to the car to get the $1800 infrared pad they will sleep on because the room is freezing and they have the $1800 infrared pad, try to repair the girl, feebly, but try.

"Are you in school?"

"Eleventh grade."

Figure out a way to compliment her intelligence, which may not be vast but which looks vast insofar as the girl is still with this mother and therefore has the patience of Job and you think that her intelligence must somehow be as large as or nearly as large as her suffering.

"You're in the IB program?"

"The whole school is sort of an IB program, it's a magnet school."

Ah. And so how to rescue her? Lock the door on the mother in the yard? No: just stand there, thinking of Woody Allen and Roman P. Keep your eye on this girl for the next two days and see if you can do anything for her. You are an ass and this girl has had enough of assness but maybe you can slide something her way that will not be more assness. You will have your hands full with the mother, but still. Even tonight you will be up until midnight hearing about the spiritual healers in Sarasota Florida the mother is referring you to, while the daughter sleeps in the cold room. Listen to the ecologically ferocious mother's twenty-minute shower from the safety of your own bed. You have told her about your own adventure with Jesus a few years ago and you may need Him again. You have withheld from her how He wears a dirty Pink Panther costume and gives bj to French husbands on family holiday. It will be interesting to see yourself try to tell her this; it will require your knowing that Jesus himself is witnessing your telling her this and chuckling at you as you do it. You must tip your hat to Jesus: when they say He is The Man, they are not kidding.

It's a new day: act like it. Put the behind behind. Appreciate the lunacy of that, of all advice. Just have a look at *appreciate* itself. If you inspect the weirdness of all advice, of the imploration that it be followed, you might have a look at the advisability, the integrity, the tenability of the imperative mood itself. Now that we have, just bag it.

Cross the stream. Build a small perfectly shaped teepee-style Boy Scout campfire and watch it burn and put it out when you are done according to standard overkill practices so that if the woods burn down tomorrow you will be blameless, even in your own head. Recall how you have felt the times you have inadvertently burnt the woods down and appreciate that this feeling clear of guilt for having redundantly shoveled a fire apart even after you have drowned it twice will be a stronger good feeling, the freedom from the guilt, than the strong dumb feeling you have had doing all that nonsense to the fire. While having the strong dumb feeling knocking apart and drowning the tiny gratuitous fire that was not even that much fun to have sat beside and watched, look around the woods for the absent wildlife. Strain your ears; hear the flutter of a sparrow or a finch, and know that you can't, but some people can, identify that bird by that flutter alone. Marvel at how some people became smart and some who once fancied themselves smart, that would be you, never were smart and never became smart, coasting along all that time without need to become smart because of the presumption that they (you) already were. You may even want to confess that you identified presumers of this sort with your best scorn until you joined the club. The appropriate expression for this surmise is "Shit." You may go ahead now and say it, by the little late fire in the wee noise of the lone fluttering bird, aloud in the woods.

The Indicative Mood

I have read that half the bees are missing. There is a woman on French TV with glossy pink cream on her lips. Oh, surely that is not called cream. Right you are, it is called gloss. So say it again. No. You have slipped into the imperative mood. All right. You have seen a woman with not cream but gloss on her lips. Yes, I have seen a woman on French TV who has glossy pink gloss on her lips. How stupid I sound. The gloss is stupid—relax. You have slipped again. Stay in the indicative. You too. I will.

What about the bees? I will not respond to that. Okay: Tell me about the bees. I will not respond to that. Okay: that half the bees are missing is interesting and possibly alarming but perhaps some details could help us along. The bees have just not come home. Your bee farmers are opening up hives and they are empty. Give me some wine. No. I would like some wine. Okay.

An early car such as a Model-T Ford or a Model-A Ford was a simple thing and it had enough room around the engine that you could stand inside the hood and fix it. And the engine was simple enough that you could fix it. Now the bees are gone. We have come a long way in the wrong direction, or in a wrong direction, I think it fair to say. There is not space inside a car hood now for a bee to work, and half the bees are MIA. I love the category MIA. It means dead but we are too pusillanimous to say so. God*damn* that is a cute girl out there on the street.

There is butter in parts of the world that has crystals of salt suspended in it. There is butter in parts of the world that has no salt in it.

This deal wherein the women have to be covered up—I am not down with it. I have patience for perversity but for a person to have to walk around under a blanket just does not position itself well in my I-can-see-that scope. My I-can-see-that scope in fact does not have in its field of view people covered up unless it is dark at night and cold in the room and they want the covers on them. I am sorry. I have refocused my scope and I just can't get that to come into view.

I love a well engineered car even if a bee cannot get under the hood. You have got to admit they run better than they did in 1930. I concede you that ground but I maintain still that we have won the battle and lost the war. I will not contest you on that. The wine is good. We want more of it. We do. We are wine wanters. We are wanters. We want shit. We do. This is good. A boy is always praised for a good appetite. No one is praised for a poor appetite. A good appetite gets one in trouble later in life, and a poor appetite would have one be lean and healthy, trim as a garter snake on a log over a creek 200 yards from a family picnic. I went once to a social put on by a club called something like the Toasters. Someone's backyard was devoted to passing out ice cream to the entire neighborhood. There were vats of ice cream of all stripe in commercial coolers in the yard. It was a riot of bloating and running and headfreeze and a weird happy panic among us who thought surely we were crashing this thing, before we knew that term, but surely we were uninvited and were going to be stopped from eating this ice cream, which we ate all the more indiscriminately for this fear of impending probation. I like the way you ended that with *probation*. Yes, it is not the precise word I wanted but I was in a rush insofar as that sentence looked capable of going on forever to end it, and possibly probation serves well precisely because it is not the right word but evokes a fuzzy neighborhood of possibility for the right word into which the audience can insert the right word. The audience are good people. I love *good people*. Me too.

If I knew anything about weaving, and had me a setup, I would weave me a good rug today. I just feel like having a good rug under construction, and later like walking on something solidly built and durable and good under the feet and good to look at as you cross it and good to look at still after you have crossed it and sat down in a good leather chair with maybe your whiskey under a pleasant yellow cone of lamplight and a not smelly dog right nearby. I can even see crossing back over this rug and signaling the dog to come on and putting on boots and getting your shotgun and going out into the field and walking with the shotgun breached over your arm and flushing two quail and glancing at the dog, who looks from the quail to you, with a small raise of his brow at your not having fired at the quail, and you say to him, or her, Those birds flew away, didn't they?, and the dog just resumes the walk. I can see all this. I wish I had a loom. The other stuff—the whiskey, the lamp, the estate with quail on it—would all fall into place. Yes it would. Like dominoes. Like world-class high-living self-important-but-not-so-important-that-we-do-not-know-how-to-be-a-modest-gentleman dominoes.

I don't think a compound modifier of that absurd a dimension is actually legitimate in the indicative mood. I don't care. Well if we are to bend rules we might as well break rules. Oh, no, that is not true. That is not the case. I would say, "Don't go jumping to seclusions," except it is imperative and not that funny. That look that the dog gives the gentleman in denial who modifies his dominoes queerly—that look contains an essence we are after and cannot state. Look—a well clad family on the street! I will not respond to that. Point taken.

The dog sees the birds flush an instant or more after he has smelled them sitting there in the bush like roasting hens. The birds blow up just off the ground in this agreeable burst of flavor and noise, and then get some air inside their feathers making the entire place smell like bird hay, and sit there generating the sufficient energy and correct air pressure for an actual flight that will carry them out of reach of his mouth, and the click of metal and the explosion that usually immediately signals birds being in this dog's mouth does not happen. The dog follows the flight of the birds and his gaze comes to rest on the man in a smooth unbroken arc, not unlike the way one moves his fingers through his hair after someone has declined to shake one's hand.

You mean the dog does not follow the birds one way until they are out of sight and then snap his head back at the man as if to say What the fuck you sumbitch did you do that for? I will not respond to that. Point taken, I will reform it: the dog looks smoothly from the disappearing birds to the man in one motion, almost like an eyeroll. Yes. Like the time we saw that girl go into the seizure who we thought was just rolling her eyes. Somewhat like that. My point is she appeared to be doing one thing with her eyes and then it proved she was really doing something else. And in just this way the dog appears to be following the quail and then he is looking at the man, with one eyebrow raised. The eyebrow raised says, What did you not shoot for? Oh, yes, and it says more than that. It says, Why are you not a man? It says, You are not a gentleman with an estate with quail on it with a whiskey back at the house that will need be refreshed near where I lie not on the stupid rug which feels much better than the wood floor, you do not even have the house or the whiskey or the lamp or the rug, you are just a boob who thinks he wants to weave a rug. He says, Who do you think you are, a Senator from Mississippi?.

Dogs never roll their eyes. That is their chief appeal to man. If you could get a dog that would do an eyeroll, and you were convinced it was always at the expense of others and not at your own expense—*man*! The eyeroll dog would set a new pace in dogs, would it not? Not accepted. The eyeroll dog would set a new pace in dogs. You could make a million dollars with a dog that would roll its eyes. It's a niche wide open.

Losing the Wax

How did I go from being full of bluster and cheer to being empty and afraid? Usually a man has to be incarcerated, or see his fellows slaughtered, or lose a child, or ... doesn't he? Normally, in a normal person, yes, I think a blow of some sort would be required to install the fearful void where there had been the hale stand-and-deliver. But a coward may just lose his sheen, as it were, and precipitate into his true state, overnight, or over a few nights, or over some modest period of time, without any sudden cause. The sheen after all was false, a gloss, like the thin wax sprayed on an apple.

The wax wears off. Spots appear, the flesh softens, consumers (friends, lovers) back off, and one is taken from the top shelf, even if just in his mind, and is headed for a bag to be sent to the sauce factory. One defense is a commensurate loss of mind, which will allow the sodden apple to be giddy about the soddening. The commensurate loss of mind can be voluntary, as a tactic of camouflage or diversion, or it may too come naturally as a contingent wearing off of essentially the same wax. At any rate the empty, afraid, ex-hale, post-stand-and-deliver fool will not accept at first that his wax is gone and that he is in decline. And then he will.

Marbles

I am sitting here without my marbles together, envying other people sitting where they are sitting with their marbles together. I have in mind a certain poet in New York, seventy-five or so, in his apartment knowing all that he knows, arranging some lines on paper that advance evidence he knows yet a little more than the prodigious sum we already knew he knew.

Bebek

Bebek up the way is so green that I start weeping. Why on earth would a spectrally green village on the Bosphorus, in a country not mine, make me weep? Do I really mean weep? Or was I not just blubbering, or chortling sad, chuckleheadedly morose, and perhaps not over Bebek or its green but over something else— like my lost loves, all the girls gone, the women who've woken up and left? Perhaps I was snotting up for those numberless waves, triggered by the improbably fresh green of trees along blue water. They've taken their underwear and gone, Captain. Let us make eggs, then.

It is not that Bebek is green but that the green is containing so much yellow, suggesting perhaps that the trees are artificial, possibly high-quality synthetic trees, that makes me burst into tears. But I burst into tears less than I . . . crumble into tears. I see these bright trees, who knows but that they are not Robert Penn Warren's infamous arsenical green, off-color in a way that suggests they are fake, or under klieg lights, which suggests deep down that Bebek is Miami, which is a globalization crime of the first order, and I begin to blubber. Blubber, and wander toward the phony trees or the trees that are so well lit and real that they look unreal, and blather. The uncertainty as to whether the trees are spectrally real or spectrally unreal is enough to make a sane man cry, and I am not a sane man. The last moment I was arguably sane was in the sixth grade. I could spell, I could impress the teacher, I thought I was the smartest boy in the room—already, alas, the seed of lunacy was present. I was never sane. Are infants sane? If they are, when, at what moment, does the bending begin? Is it a pang of hunger not satisfied immediately, a pang of hunger satisfied too soon? Is it a soiling of the body? Is it the assault of phenomena impossible to comprehend—like plastic-looking trees?

Yesterday I was sitting in my golf cart not golfing but reading when I saw peripherally an orange thing moving that I expected would prove a tabby cat, odd out in the field where I had parked the cart in the sun to read. It was not a cat but a fox, trotting at a good smooth clip, a bright yellowy fox on his way past with business on his mind. His big puffy tail followed him straight out. His pencil legs were a scissoring little blur. His head did not bounce but glided a foot above the ground on a perfect level line. He was indeed tabby-cat-orange, or -yellow. I gave him a little kissing noise which made him speed up to relative cover and distance, where he stopped and regarded me, and then resumed his course, perceptibly a little more quickly than before. This fox was entirely sane.

Hoping Weakly

I have spent some time this morning cleaning the gradu from the thumb notches on my Randall Number 23 knife. That occupied most of my mind for the duration of the cleaning. A small portion of my brain was left over with which to speculate simultaneously that I will be non-productive if I take a sabbatical next year, that I am in fact non-productive now. Which is why the bulk of my brain is engineering how to run a fingernail back and forth in the thumb-notch grooves cleaning out the gradu. The gradu itself is most likely actually metal polish with which I have idly polished the knife itself when similarly occupied by nothing better to do than shine up an already shiny knife.

Now that I have declared myself idle I have time and inclination to look out the window and appreciate the weather. The sky contains heavy low blue flat clouds slowly sliding to the north and looking like rain. I have heard some thunder. The humidity is high enough to have wilted the banded water snake skin I have that I dumbly left draped over a table edge the last time the humidity was high enough to wilt the skin. When that humidity evaporated, if you may speak of evaporation with respect to humidity, the skin of course crisped out and preserved the angle of drapage. I have been waiting for a bout of new high humidity to allow the skin to relax and flatten out and today I have it, and the skin is limp and restored, and it was touching the Randall Number 23 when I found it, and I took up the knife expecting to see salt contamination where the skin had touched it. I saw no salt damage but I did see the gradu of old polish in the thumb notches so I have applied my energies and resources, nearly all of them, to its removal.

There is a woman down at the dojo where I work out who stopped coming in because she became a real-estate agent and I miss her. She was forty-three, I believe, and in perfect shape. Her body fat does not, or did not, exceed five percent, I would have guessed. There are certain exercises in a dojo in which you have occasion to touch a partner and it was a pleasure to touch this woman. I do not mean this in a precisely sexual way or in a precisely nonsexual way. If there is a neutral interface between sexual and nonsexual, I mean that. When you touch this woman you feel either pure muscle or muscle with bone close under it or just bone itself and you want to squeeze her a bit as if to say, Good for you, girl. And if you did slip up and actually say that, and I think I might have here and there, she would not take offense but would know the remark to be a high compliment, and she would know she worked hard for someone to feel only that muscle and bone and that you knew how hard she worked and that it, muscle and bone and nothing else, was such a good and rare thing that a man could be forgiven for misspeaking or for letting his grip linger longer than absolutely required in the exercise. If the exercise called for striking one's opponent, she could be struck as hard as you'd strike a man. If it called for an excruciating number of abdominal contractions in, say, a tandem sit-up exercise called a cockpit, you would have to work very hard to keep up with her and not be embarrassed by your not keeping up with her. Now she is selling houses and there is no one at the dojo to feel thrilled by touching.

I wonder if there is a correlation in real estate between the body fat of the agent and the commission the agent pulls down. If the two are directly proportional Peggy will have to put on weight. If the relationship is, by some freak chance in a land that worships sugar, inversely proportional, then Peggy is already retired. Were she already retired, I would see her back at the dojo. I presume. I hope.

I hope for something. It is not a strong hope. The strength of the hope does not exceed—I am now seeing lightning out the window—let me restart this sentence. The weak hope I have is congruent to the weak vision I have of whatever it is I hope for. I hope weakly and vaguely. The weakness matches perfectly the vagueness. I would think that this proportionality is the best arrangement. If one hoped very hard for something one could define very well, it would be okay except for the chance of high disappointment. If one hoped very hard for something one could not define, the chance of disappointment it seems to me would be exceedingly high, if not guaranteed. If one hoped very weakly for something one could define, I would ask what is the point of hoping weakly for that which you see strongly. I hope weakly for that which I see weakly. I'll be okay no matter what.

Gluing Wood

Today we want to glue some wood to some wood. We will get all the surfaces clean with sanding and then by wiping the wood with our coarse brown paper toweling, which itself is limp wood. We will apply the good wood glue, which is the color of banana pudding, to both surfaces, liberally, and align the pieces and press them together. Before the final fit it is important to slide the pieces back and forth just a bit, or twist them a bit, depending on the configuration of the pieces; this lateral friction, as it were, is to displace small pockets of air that may be trapped in the glue if the pieces of wood merely come together head-on. Once we have a good airless fit with plenty of squeezeout we should wipe the excess glue with more paper and clamp the pieces firmly together or effect a clamping by means of weight upon the pieces. Clamping can also be effected by tying the pieces together, often with bungees. The pressure should be that of a very firm handshake. Wood being married to wood likes a good handshake. If there is more squeezeout it may be addressed after this clamping or the dried excess glue may be sanded off later. You can use your anytime minutes on small squeezeout. If one of you would go get me a Musketeers the morning would be better. Some of you know how I put a Musketeers in a Dr. Pepper and how the acid in the Dr. Pepper will make the Musketeers into something like a very tasty sea slug. Which if it goes too long though it can be difficult to lift it out in one piece. I call that the Drooping Musketeer and I don't really like it, I don't. At a certain point you have to just stir the Musketeer into the Dr. Pepper. A Baby Ruth looks like a turd. A Butterfinger is wont to explode. Never recap your Dr. Pepper if you are using Butterfinger. I must tell you that because the Surgeon General won't. The cleaning industry tells you not to combine its stuff but the candy industry does not. If there is no caution statement on a candy bar telling you that it is bad for your health in several ways, chief among them obesity and Type 2 diabetes, it is not finally surprising that they not tell you that under certain conditions the candy unit will explode and perhaps blow your pop bottle apart and blind you, or worse. The good wood glue we use here is pretty set up in an hour. Tomorrow we will start in on the router. The router is essential but many a one thinks it is just some kind of dangerous cosmetic tool. It is not. Get your wood and get to gluing and stop wasting time.

The Retarded Hermit

The hermit knew he was illiterate but had not thought, in the beginning, that illiterate necessarily also imputed retarded. As he got deeper into the hermitage, and more dim-witted when he infrequently ran into people, he began to sense that retardation was actually part of the deal with him. He realized that he had always been stupid but that his energy as a youth had been sufficient that he had been able to mask stupidity with avidity. As his avidity waned he saw clearly the stupidity that had been underneath it all along, like the mud flat that is under a receding tide. The happy frisky bright blue waters drew slowly off, leaving a dull flat plain of mud. This was his brain.

His next realization on this score was that he was so retarded, in fact, that the discovery of a mud flat in his head did not overly bother him, except for the embarrassment of having thought himself not stupid most of his life. He had had little tolerance for people who overrated themselves in this regard, and now he had to admit that he had been among the worst of the presumers. But with an admission of stupidity can come an admission of amnesia when it is convenient, so he conveniently forgot that he had once presumed himself smart, and he became more and more comfortable in the fact that he was dumber than a post-horse on radio day. That was the kind of locution that might strike him in the new fulgent retardation, and he would happily use such a locution notwithstanding that it meant nothing. It did mean something: it meant he was in fact stupid if he used it, as stupid as a post-horse on radio day. As stupid as a lean killing machine on Tuesday. As stupid as a cloud. Dumber than God on the day he made incense.

How had he become a hermit? It was difficult to recall. If he tried to recall, he might come up with something like this: I met a girl who told me she had made a fortune making other women believe that the gizmo she sold them would effortlessly fry the fat off their ass. He would say also: That's the way she put it, which for some reason really made me laugh: "Fry the fat off their *ass!*" I would see one ass, one quantity of fat, millions of women buying this gizmo.

In fact the hermit had met no such woman. If he tried to recall how he had become a hermit he might deliver himself of other fictions as well. A dog told him to become a hermit. As a hermit he would be able to position himself eventually to repudiate plumbing and be a natural man. As a hermit he would never have the means to deliberately go to an air show, and it was probable that one would never accidentally come to him. The problem of not having enough bricks of the right color was never going to trouble him, if he became a hermit. And so forth.

So he became more comfortable with however he had become what he'd become, and more comfortable with the realization that what he had most become was stupid. People not speaking to him, which had once worried him when it developed, now served as a kind of validation. He liked them over there not speaking, as opposed to over here causing trouble with their attentions in which he was not that interested and which he could not comprehend anyway in his fast-draining neap-tide stupidity. My head so out of water, he said one day, I can see fiddlers running in and out of they tiny holes. He wanted to talk like a Mississippi blues man but knew that that too was a pose of intellection that he could not sustain. Those guys were smart enough to all sound the same way, to talk in a code of agreed-upon stylization to fool the doofus acolytes. He did not really have any such theories about Mississippi blues men duping their congregation or want to talk like one. It was just another kind of lie that drifted through his head, across the mudflat of his brain, as agreeable as any other lie. He had no idea what a post-horse was, if there even was such a thing. There was some logic to faulting God for making incense, but he had no idea what might be meant by a radio day. This was the essence of the new condition: nonsense now made sense as he realized the sense he had insisted upon had never actually made sense. His life had become a fabric of tiny lies instead of a construction of some truths and verities around which some lies might buzz. His life was all a buzzing lie, and it always had been. In one way, once this stopped alarming you, it made you very happy. It took the pressure off. It was like skydiving without leaving the house, or even one's chair.

It was time, in this new condition, to get a good tank of fish and send off to Russia for a mail-order bride. He would like a school of lipstick-red platys and a Ukrainian girl named Elena. She was thirty-six and had a boy eight years old. She skied and reported that she tried to keep fit. She did not describe herself bizarrely as the younger women tended to. ("It is difficult to judge myself but

I can describe myself as trustful, emotional, calm, serious, tidy, purposeful, friendly, sincere, thrifty, sexy, patient, persistent, sacrificial, responsible, accurate, and honest. I have a lot of friends who say that I am communicative, modest, sensitive, sentimental, calm, democratic, reasonable, romantic, sympathetic, womanly, and economical woman.") All Elena said was "I'm warm-hearted, communicative, tender, kind, and loving. I like traveling, picnics with my friends in the open air. I adore skiing. I try to keep fit." Would he no longer be a hermit if he secured these fish and this bride? He would be a hermit with some fish who did not talk and with a Russian bride who did not talk much, apparently, so in a way, he thought, taking the perspective from outside, he would be even more of a hermit than he now was. The hermit has taken a bowl of fish and a silent Russian wife, they would say down in the village or wherever it was that people discussed hermits. It was a fine plan. But it was not a fine plan.

It would require energy to acquire a bowl of fish and a bride, even one by mail-order. He could perhaps, if she was to deliver herself to the door—he did not know how it worked, but something this easy was going to be necessary—ask her to pick up the fish on the way. This idea was appealing but it caused the first fear associated with the plan. These Russian women had spunk and did not want to marry a layabout or a retarded person, that much was clear from their ambitions and desires in the catalog profiles. They seemed like good soldiers in this regard: rugged, ready to work, to party, and expecting their comrades in the trench to be good heads beside theirs. It did not bode well in his imagination, even as low-tide as it was, to tell such a woman to get fish along the ten-thousand-mile journey unto him and to then unwrap herself and present herself to him without his getting up off the bed, which is how he saw this all happening in the mudflat of his brain. This fish-and-bride plan was a non-starter.

Language of that sort had once irritated him. That's a non-starter and I'm a self-starter so it's not copacetic with *moi*. But now to say something was a non-starter was a delight. He himself was a non-ender. He was not in the middle of anything either. Oh, Elena, he said to no one, not even really to himself, and arguably not even to her phantom self ten thousand miles away keeping fit in Ukraine: Oh, Elena, I'd make you a good man if I were a different man, but as it is you'd get here on radio day and little Sergei—is he eight?—would want to play soccer and I'd have to take him down to Little League, if I could even find it, and he'd wind up on the crummy team for boys who can't play, as I wound up, and then he'd be headed for a life not unlike his mad stepfather's and he would come to long even more than he does now for his real Ukrainian father, and you, well your own disappointments would accrue just as certainly and vigorously, and, besides, I am older than the age range you say you want your partner to fall within and would have to petition for an extension of about ten years, and I would ask you to get some tropical fish on the way, just like step out of line after customs and pick some up, and it would be hard with your "with-dictionary" English level for me to explain what a lipstick-red platy is, and how disappointing it is that all they have now are these swordfish-orange platys, so you really have to look hard, maybe go to twenty tropical-fish shops in brand-new huge and confusing America en route to the hermit's lair and still probably not find lipstick-red fish, so, really, and also, I am retarded now, so really I think it better that you stay in Ukraine with Sergei and wait for a better offer from a better man. I hope you agree.

The New World

In the New World we went our Separate Ways. There's a rat in separate. In the New World large colorful fruit hung from trees, and pink piglets trotted about cleaning up the downfall. There was consequently no smell of rot, or fruit flies, and these piglets did not seem to mature and be seen as gross adults wallowing in mud or otherwise stinking up the place. Just cute pink pigs scarfing up the red and green and yellow fruit on the ground and running off before any of it came out of them the other way. When I first apprehended this system of fruit disposal by permanently cute pigs who do not defecate in your presence it occurred to me that I must be in a Utopia with a good mind at the helm—nay, a superior mind. I gave my wife all the credit cards, putting them into a pistol holster I had had lying around, and she went over the dale happily, armed. I thought for a moment she resembled a horse going over the horizon, agreeably clopping her Separate Way with a bouncy if clumsy gait. There was nothing to be bought in the New World with the credit cards, or with anything else other than your luck or your charm. She knew this, or I thought she knew this, but having all the credit cards nonetheless made her happy, and I was happy to have made her happy, for once. After all, Separate Ways would not have been obtaining unless there had been failure in this dimension, The Making Happy of the Other. It is of course the final dimension, and accordingly the most difficult to negotiate successfully. You enter this dimension usually without having mastered the other, preceding impossible dimensions, such as Tumescence at the Right Time. Here's a good saying: He (or she, or it) is not worth the powder it would take to blow him.

I became a trotting-horse racer in the New World. I was walking by the track and a fellow I was afraid was going to try to panhandle me or sell me drugs or a girl said, "Much you weigh, mon?" to which I said, "Say what?"

"If you not over one fitty, come scrate wit me now at dis time immediately."

I was put on a scale and then put in a cart and a bell rang and a horse pulled me around a track and I was handed fifty, or fitty, dollars. I do this twice a week on Wednesday and Saturday afternoons. My style has developed as an imitation of what I did, apparently successfully, that first time: I just hold the reins lightly on the horse's back. No urging or cajoling. The horse wants to run or he doesn't. I concentrate only on staying in the cart and keeping my little helmeted head level. I admire the other drivers' more active styles, but that's not for me, in the New World. I am called El Placido. My colors are pink and black and green. I watch my weight. The cart and the harness tack is well made and I admire it. It smells good and feels good and heavy. At speed in a race there is a good breeze in your face and there is a good quantity of mud and dirt aflyin'. It's all good. I do not smile inauthentically in the New

World. Here's a good saying: So-and-so has enough money to burn a dead mule.

Friendlies, or family-friendly things, or something like that. I dreamed a fellow saying or writing something like this. It was of course to have meant something, and perhaps it would, or would have, were I to recall exactly what the fellow wrote or said, but I do not. I do not because my mind is shot. In the New World, as in the Old, it pays to secure a position that a shot mind does not impeach or imperil but in fact enhances and aggrandizes. Thus I keep my head very level in the horse trotting. Here's a good saying: No human sorrow ever stopped the world.

From a fellow with one hand at a market I purchased a box of parrots. They looked up like puppies when you peeked in. I got them home and opened the four box-top flaps completely and let the birds fly out. I opened all the doors and windows. All but two birds more or less straightaway left the building. One clung to a cornice and said something very close to "Polly want a cracker." I will be making a supreme effort to hear this more clearly if it is repeated and to find crackers here in the New World. The other bird that stayed in the house perched on my shoulder, which delighted me. He bit my earlobe very hard, I thought certainly removing it, and I flinched and somewhat swatted at him, and he fluttered and puffed out his feathers and gave a loud caw, and then rather primly and ceremoniously readjusted his feet on my shoulder and looked me in the eye, evenly, as if to say "My bad," and he has not tried to eat my earlobe again, if that is in fact what he tried to do, or was thinking of doing. My experience with parrots is early but I see that it may prove hard to ascribe motive with them. Was it a bite of some kind of vengeance? Was he off his rocker from being boxed like a puppy? Is he in love with me and unaware of his strength? I believe him to be aware of his strength because I have seen him bite through a tin can since the earlobe adventure. Here's a good saying: The New World may be in fact a very, very, very, very Old World.

On purchasing in the New World: as I have intimated previously, this is a curious operation. The credit cards my wife happily bounded over hill and dale with are useless, as is cash, had she any. Moreover, most strangely, outright bartering or trading also seems to be not done. I got the parrots, for example, by merely looking curiously at them through the slits in the box top, lining up their small bright eyes with mine, and eventually also lining up my eyes with those of the proprietor of the parrot business, the man sitting beside the box of parrots. He gently pushed the box toward me and gave a very slight backhand gesture near the box that clearly said, Take it away. Nothing was required of me but that I comply, and the sense was palpable that a large social error of some sort would have resided in my not complying. I take it that the parrot man can go look at something that attracts him or that he needs and it will similarly be made his, and that at some point I too will make this dismissive gesture regarding something I have that someone has lingered upon for a moment. It is a rather thrilling non-commercial commerce and I hope it works. Here's a good saying: Do not be in too big a hurry to lick the red off your candy.

At the track they told me my silks needed pressing and that a girl would be by my place to attend to it. The next day a young woman named Evita arrived and put the place in tip-top shape, bed made, floors spotless, the silks hung on a wire, a bowl of bright fruit, giant camellias floating in a dish. She showed me around with some pride as if it were a place new to me, which it was. I said, "Mighty tidy," which phrase Evita repeated, apparently not comprehending but liking it. She got on the bed and patted it next to her. I lay down with her and she instituted unapologetic and hungry carnality. The bed was mussed and she got up and put it to rights and left. Here's a good saying: Apply shingles from the bottom up.

I am a member of the Country Club for Revolutionaries Only. The clubhouse is of unpainted cinder block and about twelve feet by twenty feet, a bar and a few tables. We drink but water. The members speak of scoring well or not scoring well, happily, but there is no golf course. Nor is there a tennis court or a pool or any property whatsoever outside, as near as I can tell. We toast to the revolution, we share the water, we speak of shooting well or not well, happily. There is another club in town sometimes spoken of: the Country Club for Those Who Mourn Lost Spouses. There is a latent note of derision when mention of this club is made, and an almost tacit tongue-clucking that says the sons of bitches over there (playing actual golf and drinking booze), as opposed to the sons of bitches over here (playing phantom golf and drinking water), do not know what they are doing. Here's a good saying: What goes around comes around.

My two parrots, the two who stayed with me—Polly, usually on the cornice, to whom I closely listen for another pronouncement upon wanting a cracker, and the other, mostly on my shoulder, who seems now to tease me by feinting at my earlobe—I have noticed are colored exactly as are my racing silks, green and black and pink. That this coincidence, or very opposite of coincidence, took me so long to notice is disturbing. It forces me to wonder if the parrots who escaped were colored differently and if the non-alignment, as it were, of their colors is what persuaded them to fly away. It forces me to ponder the question of coincidence, which I see in Darwinian terms, or not: is the likeness of my birds and my colors a kind of natural selection, or is it a sign that there is a designing instrument in our midst? When I am in my silks it appears that there are three birds in my bungalow, one of them larger and less bright. Here's a good saying: Don't hesitate to insulate your house, especially the floor.

When I spot my wife at a distance gamboling freely over hill and dale there is a small throating of sadness. I wish I had been smarter at marriage. I was not altogether smart. It is, a divorce, not unlike bringing a meal along slowly and then through neglect burning this dish or that, and then perhaps another, and ultimately facing the situation, after long work, of an inedible repast, guests milling around unsatisfied and ready to head out for fast food. All that was needed was an ounce or two more of circumspection and caution and witness. The vision of the ruined meal will linger.

Yesterday at the market I saw a bright and well-fed child with a parrot on her shoulder. I have not ventured out of doors with mine. I inquired of the child why her bird did not fly away. "Because his wings are clipped," she said, in a crisp British accent.

"And he knows that?" I asked.

"Yes," she said, confident of this intelligence. "He sticks his head in my mouth," she added, as if to bolster the case for the knowingness of her bird. She opened her mouth and turned to the bird, which did incline his head into her mouth.

"He eats from there."

"You put seed on your tongue?"

"No, food, when I'm chewing." The bird looked at me as if to suggest I was not quite with it. The child was looking elsewhere, through with my not being with it.

I was comfortable with not being with it. That is a function, I think, of the New World: not only is angst for being out of it gone, the matter is somewhat to be chuckled at that one ever fretted about being in the know, about anything. Here's a good saying: It is quite all right to put all the eggs in one basket if you *watch that basket*.

Today there was a roundup of the cute pink pigs. They were assembled into the town square and told to sit and they did, like dogs. They were examined by a person in a white coat whom I took to be a veterinarian but who I also suspected was merely a person in a white coat, perhaps a steward's coat from a ship. At the terminus of each examination he whistled and a child came from the surrounding audience and gave the pig completing his examination a candy bar. This the pig deftly unwrapped with clever hooves that surprised me, and devoured swiftly—-"devoured swiftly" is archaic-sounding but perfectly apt. The pig then also spoke to the child: "Thank you, sir," or "Thank you, madam." Most of the children bowed or curtsied then to the pig. What was most startling in this perhaps hallucinatory vision was not the dexterity of the unwrapping or the pigs' speaking in human tongue but their use of these terms "sir" and "madam" and the formal bowing and curtsying by the children. These were things I thought from the Old World and I did not know how or why they got in the New World, and why they would be regarded fondly, these old manners. The pigs, when all had been examined and fed, were dismissed, and I came to realize I had just witnessed some kind of mythological, or myth-making, amalgam of ritual: of, say, The Three Pigs (With No Wolf) and Halloween. There seemed an affinity between this affair without its wolf and its costumes and my country club without its golf and its liquor; in the New World we made a strength of absence. Everyone was much pleased with this afternoon of nice pigs and manners.

I trot in pink and green flying silks, I cavort with Evita on crisp white sheets, I see pigs behave, I have not a trouble in the world, I despair. What is it about me? Is it the shadow of the gamboling ex-wife, the retardation that having a gamboling ex-wife suggests? As a human being, I realize, I am a nubbin. The pigs are ambassadors next to me. They take candy from children with grace. Could I yet perhaps learn, myself, how to behave?

I lay down in front of the bungalow as it started to rain and observed, for hours, the square foot or so of dirt before my head. I saw a preponderance of animals so small I was not sure they were not grains of the soil, and indeed the matter of classifying animal/vegetable/mineral became a task beyond me as the earth was bombarded by the huge and fat explosions of rain pocking the ground. Once a centipede hove into view. Three segments of a worm bent into and out of sight. An ant was struck by a drop of rain and shook his head to clear it. The dirt itself moved, buoying the lighter components of itself up, the heavier down, and migrating onto my face. Evita came and picked me up. She put me in the shower and braced me against a wall of it with her forearm and washed me roughly with a rag, as if I were a dog. She put us to bed and lay with me gently and said, "I am Our Lady of Eternal Succor." Polly was up on the cornice as if she were observing us and I thought it a perfect time for her to say, a second time, if in fact she said it the first time, that she wanted a cracker, but Polly did not open her mouth.

Evita is most tender and I continue to regard Polly, and Polly us, and I cop an epiphanic glow. I have a tincture of an inkling of a good saying, and suddenly see that a good approach, instead of waiting for a bird to say something again that it might not have already said, is to assume that a bird wants a cracker whether it can say so or not, and to get your ass up and give a bird a cracker and ask yourself, motivationally, just what the hell is wrong with you that you have not been providing all birds crackers with all you have. A good saying: in a New World behave in a new way as a new man. Unhorse the conquistador.

Wagons, Ho!

Wagon boss: Today there are fewer Indians than before. Clouds are swaying up there in the big sky like the bellies of belly dancers. Our teeth feel loose. We are not possessed of resolve. We wonder if the same doubt has seized the red man. We do not think of him as often subject to doubt. The idea of him in his teepee cowering from a want of self-confidence disturbs us as much or more than the idea of our own cowering. We are not afraid of him, mind you, but of something less tangible that we cannot name. It is precisely the murkiness of this fear that makes it disturbing. Alas, I suppose I am saying we fear fear itself far more than a thing to be feared. As cornball as that may sound, I am afraid it is true. We do not fear resolve, right or wrong, but we are made much uncomfortable by want of resolve. It is easy to understand in this light how General Custer appeared so delighted at the end. The music was about to stop playing for him and his band, but until it did his needle was in the groove.

The only party not unhappy in this camp is Cook, who pounds away at something too hard to eat in its native state and all day has in his brain the notion *delicious*. Or maybe the notion is *good enough that these bastards will not complain within earshot.* Either way, he beats food with resolve. We sit here without.

We will need move all these wagon wheels, broken or not, over here, and leave those skulls alone, and push these tiara sets into the woods. (We never contest the unfathomable on the Inventory; the labor required to fill out Form 0009.09, Derequisitioning Items on the Inventory for Which No Earthly Use Can Be Divined, dwarfs the labor to carry the unfathomable to California; we can possibly use the tiaras for a Little Miss Prairie Beauty Contest; possibly put them on the bulls for a rodeo.) We will be firm with our untoward and uncharitable desires, and forsake fresh meat, and be so incredibly generous with children that we burst into tears and spook the children, and fear the Indians but never show it, except as we run like hell, and just in general I think we are ready to accede that it is all pretty much too much for us, the ordnance questions, the panniers, the supply lines, the weather, the hearty meals or not and the hearty hopes or not, it's all just . . . .

Settler one: Your position, perhaps because it is so ill-defined, is certainly not for that less than eminently defensible. You have our sympathies entire.

Settler two: I might take exception to one matter within our leader's resolve manifesto. I would like one of those tiara sets before we push them into the woods. Or two. It might be nice to have a friend wear one with me. I question also the curious phrase "push them into the woods." Do we severally do this with our feet, or do we fire up the dozer, why not *hurl* them into the woods, why into the woods, why, now that I am alert to it, get rid of the tiara sets at all? Are they a liability? Why can they not be merely left alone like the skulls? If we don't want them (the tiaras, and I see no sense in not wanting them), we could even, say, put them on the skulls before we invest in the peculiar energy of by whatever means transporting them into the woods. In short, I think our leadership has gone daft. I *want* a tiara. I will herewith lead a revolt on behalf of any others who wish to have a tiara, or two, or who at least question the wisdom, for want of better term, of pushing them into the woods.

Wagon boss: The Indians have not manifested themselves on the ridge lines of the surrounding hills in such prodigious number that we lose momentarily our breath and wonder if we are not in some kind of eclipse before finding ourselves indeed in some kind of eclipse, that of our very lives in one of those maddening tomahawk storms, those hurricanes of stone and hoof and yelling paint and buckskin and blood and everyone, including ourselves, hitting us with one thing or another while we generally find it more and more difficult to breathe, more and more difficult to see, more and more difficult to stand up, more and more difficult, alas, to keep on keepin' on. The Indians have not shown us this unhappy formation and preparedness for, really, quite some time now. I wonder if it is not that collection of tiaras somehow protecting us. My order to dispose of them may be imprudent.

I have never thought about the tiara much. I have thought much about the Indian. One of the most recurring thoughts I have in that venue is of the last hurricane they put us through, which so many of us, constituting so few of the original number of us, somehow survived. I was personally on my knees, having given up; I was dementedly lining up fallen tomahawks on the ground in front of me, in an interesting head-to-tail bric-a-brac pattern, when I noticed an Indian pony go closely by me and *wink* at me. This happened then several more times, perhaps five or six, interrupting me at the business of arranging the tomahawks attractively on the ground. The pony kept winking, as if telling me that it would be all right, that this was not the disaster that it was his job to help make it all look like, that I was not to worry overmuch. So I did not, and eventually quit my brocade of tomahawks and fondly watched the revolutions of the winking pony exclusively. And here I am today, and I think now that I too would like to have a tiara. I don't think I need two. No, I don't, I don't want two. I just want the one.

All of these pelts are good to go. Had we any idea where the fur traders are we would be sitting prettier. We will be eating beaver-tail sandwiches by the estimate of the quarterback, the quartermaster, for six weeks, no exceptions.

Nearly every time we slake our thirst of the effects of the blistering sun by guzzling water from the clear cool mountain streams, face down like dogs, we discover about a hundred feet upstream something big and putrid and dead, or I should say big and dead and putrid to more accurately reflect the sequence of perception. What you first see, actually, is something *big* enough that you notice it at all, and then when it does not retreat at your approach you surmise it is *dead*, and by then you are sufficiently upon it to revel in its inevitable *putrid*ness. So we discover, every time we drink of lifesaving cool water, something big and dead and putrid in it. *And we move on*, to the music of steel and leather and oncoming gastrointestinal complaint.

I was once struck by an arrow so sharp and so deftly put in me that, after the initial sting, which I ineffectively swatted at and decided had been a large carnivorous insect of so fearful a description that I was lucky not to have seen it, I went about my day, not discovering the arrow until I reclined upon it that evening. Perhaps as many as twenty-five of my pioneer brethren and sistern may have, must have, seen this wicked protuberance from my back and said nothing, operating, I suppose, under the general directive we obey out here not to dwell on the negative.

One of the supreme difficulties of living on an advancing frontier such as ours is that we may not have dogs and cats. We try, but they, like, we guess, get lost, or decide that the nomad life is not for them and just wordlessly slip off to make more permanent homesteads along the way. We have many (unconfirmed) reports that the Indians do have dogs and cats. If so, this will be an area for investigation in the matter of final reparations and restitution in the grievance settlements.

Here is what we wear on our shirt sleeves: mud, blood, snot, not feelings. Our feelings we wear somewhere inside our vests, close to our chests, like grubs in moist wood. This is best.

The Cork

I make a good firm precise cut with the razor blade into the cork, from one side of the cork to the longitudinal axis. The cork is a segment of a cone, the diameter of one end approximately twice that of the other end, both ends flat. I am too stupid to know the name of this geometric figure and too stupid to know offhand, or even with industry, where to find out the name. "With industry" is some kind of vagueness by which I might mean crossing the room and getting the dictionary and then not knowing what to look up—cone? cork? I might mean a call to the reference desk at the library and then having to stammer, "Do you know how old-fashioned fishing corks were shaped, actually also the corks that were put into bottles as stoppers which were larger at one end than the other so that they *stopped* before going into the bottle?" And if I could get an affirmative, I would then say, "Well, what is the figure of this cork called? I need to know."

At this point the librarian would not say, "Why do you need to know?" as he, or indeed she, might want to but would be prevented from by a consideration of professionalism.

So I would not be able to say, "Oh, you know, so if I were to try to write about cutting one of these corks for the purpose of inserting into it some fishing line, I would not have to waste a lot of words in an awkward and tedious and probably unserving description of the kind of cork I am talking about, I could just name it with the obscure geometer's term that no one would know the meaning of and be done with it, and given that no one understood what kind of cork I was talking about anyway, in the absence of the long imprecise description at least he could get on with it. And there is a certain kind of person who might be bothered by not knowing the term for the cork and he might himself, if he was this kind of person, and if he was sufficiently bothered by it, go to the dictionary, but there is the other sort of person who would be unbothered by not knowing the term and just breeze on, gratified, perhaps even unconsciously, but gratified nonetheless, that he did not have to wade through the vague and tedious description of the cork which leaves him no better informed of it than the proper name which eludes him but which, the fumbling description, requires of him considerable time in the reading thereof."

The librarian I am not going to call might, yes, be a woman, and may I say here that perhaps the most beautiful woman I have ever seen is a reference librarian? A woman so beautiful that men decline the opportunity to speak to her at all, and indeed one whom I am not at complete liberty to speak to in all the ways I might wish to speak to her, by which I mean only of course all the ways, or some of the ways, chiefly the intimate ways, that a man might be expected to want to speak to a woman he regards as the most beautiful he has ever seen.

Into the cork I press the monofilament fishing line, by holding a length of it tightly as one holds dental floss and pressing it into the razored slit that describes a plane to the longitudinal center of the cork, there we've been through that quite enough I think. Now we have something to behold. We have this cork, handsome in its lines whatever they may be actually called: a nice set of circles (two) and diagonals (two in transection or 180 of them if you elected to conceive of one line per degree) connecting them, the larger end of the cork fluting down to the other, or the smaller flaring up to the larger, as you choose. The cork's surface has its agreeable mottle, its imperfections adding up to the sense of a perfect imperfectness, a phenomenon in nature (viz marble, for example) that we find very pleasing—you know, rose-mole all stipple on a trout and glory be to God for dappled things, old Hopkins was all over it. Alas, we have the humble, brindled cork, only a piece of tree bark actually, but a piece of bark machined into the demi-cone with its precision, even if our vocabulary lacks the precision to name it, and through the cork now penetrating the center of one end and emerging from the center of the other end a fine plastic line, whether greenish or bluish always suggestive of water in its color, this string from the laboratory running precisely through this thing which floats taken from the side of a tree.

Why am I on about this cork and its new alien, plastic axis? Well, for one thing, as you can tell, I find something aesthetically pleasing about its construction, its antinomies, its little ironies, even its indictment of my intellectual fundament, or perhaps I mean my epistemological grasp, by which I might mean my sense that that summer-school course in geometry following the tenth grade, which might serve as a symbol for my education entire, was not adequate. For another, this cork sits here in its pleasing contrasts telling me I might even go fishing. There, fishing, with cork upright and approximately one-half submerged, in the slim event—it is the modern world—a fish takes it down, it will displace water to a greater degree as it sinks and then upon actual submersion the water will close over the larger plane of its top with considerable force and effect a very agreeable little snap or pop, and this sound—coupled with the undiluted boyhood thrill of *game on* and the enduring surprise of seeing the cork *disappear*—will startle me in a finite and uncomplicated and most pleasing way. Something more involved and more mundane may ensue—a fish one does not want, a fish injured one does not wish to injure, one's bait robbed, etc.—but the moment of the cork in the water, at the ready, is pure. I have no need, however, of taking it fishing: I have the cork with the line through it, and that is enough. It is itself, a thing I have made. It is there. It does not bode complications. It is not a telephone, say, that is going to ring. It does not contain an assault upon me of the world and my dim access unto it.

I could now freely call the most beautiful reference librarian in the world and not ask the name of the figure of the cork. I could say, "I have a thing I do not need trouble you with the naming of. I remember you from a party. I saw you and was struck by you. You could be making a living with your looks, professionally, I mean, and I trust you do not think I am being vulgar, though I suppose I am. Let it be: I am vulgar. You could be comfortable and famous by contriving to let men, and women, look at you, as opposed to not being comfortable or famous and having men call you up and ask you the name of the figure of the cork they might be wasting their little lives playing with. I saw you and was struck by you to such a degree that the obviousness of carnality went right by us as I stepped up and talked to you, openly and cleanly, except for the fact that I correctly noticed that no other men were stepping up to talk to you because they were stuck in the carnality of their imaginings of you. You bring that on in a mortal, you effing librarian. It is just that I am a little past mortal, or not yet there. I have no doubt been there—there was a time I would have run from the room as other men, or stepped up and proposed intercourse in some properly masked fashion, but now I have reached the cork stage. I have this cork here, it is not a phone that is going to ring— and even when I say that I see a comparatively agreeable Bakelite phone of the forties with a rotary dial and five-digit numbers and a live operator you might know the first name of, not the instrument of complex tumor-bearing mind-scattering hell that a phone represents today—I have this cork, I don't have you, I want this cork, I might want you."

That would be okay, saying that, not unlike seeing the cork go down, before the ensuing mundane complications of the catch or the repudiation, the tangle of lives, the impure disentangling that is always necessary and never final.

Not Much Is Known

There are people one wants to know, and people one does not want to know, and of course people one would want to know and people one would not want to know if one met them. A few people know a lot of people, many people know a few people, and some people know just some people. It comes down to the impulse to know everyone or to know no one. It's a distillation column. At the top are the gregarious everyone-knowers, at the bottom the hermits. At the top the saints, at the bottom the killers. Some killers just want to kill one person, some want to kill hundreds or thousands. At the very bottom is a man who knows no one but himself, not well, and wants to kill himself.

He has one pair of shoes and once had a dog. The dog liked to eat ice cream from a bowl, and its impeccable house habits and grooming habits deteriorated after it was struck by a car. After that it was accidentally closed in a car in the sun and died of heat prostration and the man found the dog with its collar improbably caught in the seat springs under the car seat. He, the man, was about twelve. The dog was not, as the expression goes, still warm; the dog was very hot. The man, or boy, pulled the dog out by the collar once he got him free of the undercarriage of the seat and laid him on a patch of green grass to cool down. He went inside and reported to his mother and father that Mac was dead.

Mac was a wire-haired terrier and looked handsome there cooling in the grass. His life had been hard after the accident with the car: a pin in his hip, the shitting on the patio, the no longer having a festive taste for ice cream from a bowl. The father freshened a hole in the backyard that had been begun by the boy for an underground fort and buried Mac in it. When later he could not find his reading glasses it was theorized that they had slipped from his pocket into Mac's grave, and the mother asked the boy to dig Mac up and look for the glasses. What? the boy asked, and the mother then suggested it was not after all a good idea and desisted in the request that the boy dig the dog back up before the boy asked, as he later felt he would have, why he and not his father—who had alone conducted the burial and alone selected the depression left by the boy's abandoned fort— why he and not the father was to dig the dog up, looking for the father's, not his, glasses. The dog died trapped in a salmon-colored Renault. It was not known who closed him in it.

Not much else is known. It is not known why we become more frightened or saddened by things as we age rather than less.

Matter of Time

He would regard the objects around him and remark on
them. He would regard the objects around him and not remark
on them. He would not regard the objects around him and remark
on them. He would not regard the objects around him and not
remark on them.

These dispositions came and went, overlapping each other,
mingling equally or one dominating for a time, then the others,
in any order. But over time he came to see that he had observed
them more or less in the given order, and that they had, while
enjoying overlaps and recessions, succeeded each other like phases
of the moon. He was now not regarding things and not remarking
on them. It was agreeable but left him little to do. The difficulty,
among others, with observing and remarking on things was that
it was too much to do, as was observing and not remarking, as was
not observing and remarking anyway. So he felt that if he felt there
was too little to do in not observing things and not remarking on

them, that this was a trivial sensation that would pass and give way to the great unbusy and wise calm he was after.

Traveling from point to point was next: it was clearly, literally, pointless in the long run. In the short term it was just dailiness and the dull business of surviving the days. In surviving the days people were trying to lengthen their time on earth in order to reduce mind and body as much as possible to a skeleton before stepping into the grave. It seemed to him that that could be accomplished more elegantly and with less waste by just sitting in a good chair. "Let's get this show on the road," he said one day, the last thing he ever said, and picked his chair and sat.

For a moment he fretted the position of the chair as to whether it was in the sun or not, or in too much sun if it were in the sun, before realizing that that fretting was bootless because the sun would lower and leave him no matter where he sat, and he was not going to follow it. If he were going to follow the sun, he might as well take city buses to and fro all over the city and observe the world and issue copious remarks upon it. He might as well live a long chattering gay life before hopping into his hole all bones. He almost thought that people must be attempting, in their festive pointless frenetic living, to be gathering momentum which would carry their bones into the next world still animate. Perhaps in the next world there would be no forces to oppose the energies of a skeleton and it would, with an ounce of momentum, go on forever. That could possibly explain why people insisted on running their marathon daily lives as they did, going from point to point, eating, observing, making their points, delivering their opinions, then excuse-me resting up for tomorrow's round. They were trying to deliver their frames unto eternity with a running start. There they planned to go on chattering forever and forever gay, as clicking and clacking bones, no longer pestered by, or pestered in a different way by, weight problems. They were quite clearly trying to remain in the sun all day and all night if they could. The sun was a very symbol of what he had come to quit in quitting the regarding and the remarking and the going. He had also quit the sun.

He sat in the odd corner of the patio, then, having quit. Matter of time, he thought, matter of time. That meant more than he wanted it to mean, so rather than ponder it—a species of observing, remarking, going—he reissued it: Matter of time now, matter of time.

Matter of time.

He was perhaps not the happiest man alive, but he was, he was sure, not the unhappiest, and he thought he had a good chance of being the happiest man not alive. That was tenable, and a matter of time would tell.

Not regarding the world and not remarking on it from his chair in the sun or not in the sun was going to prove an unworkable position from which to execute his duties as a judge of circuit court, so Mr. Hollingsworth made preparations to retire. The day he did retire he came home to find one of his daughters telling him that his wife had lost her mind. His orientation and attitude in his chair required for that a momentary adjustment.

His daughter, who had never been fond of him, was now fondly showing him a drawerful of loose longhand pages that she claimed was the surest sign her mother had finally gone over the edge. He admitted to himself that that much writing under any voluntary circumstances did look suspicious, but these pages looked even odder than they might have in their condition and context. They were as beat-up as hard-used currency, and stained like cookbook pages, and had among them snapshots and birthday candles and a screwdriver. Even a glance suggested they were somehow about

Nathan Bedford Forrest, a confederate general whom he, Mr. Hollingsworth, knew something about but whom he didn't know she, Mrs. Hollingsworth, knew anything about. A second glance, which he made sitting at the kitchen table attempting to dislocate his daughter from his ear, suggested that what Mrs. Hollingsworh knew about General Forrest appeared to be entirely fanciful. He could not give his attention to the document because the daughter was now silently but desperately gesturing for him to come look through the keyhole of the bathroom door at, presumably, his wife. "She's taking *a bath!*" the daughter stage whispered, as if it were the height of outrage. He found the idea of peeping at his wife agreeable, if the daughter were not there. The entire situation here suggested that somehow his wife had also managed to take a seat in the chair of disregard that did not follow the sun. It appeared, moreover, that they had sat down simultaneously and independently in the same chair, in one another's laps as it were. They had been remote from each other for some time. This was a surprising and agreeable new intimacy, if that's what it was. For the sake of simplicity and hope in a better world, Mr. Hollingsworth decided to assume that that's what it was. He and his wife were, somehow, magically and newly intimate.

He said aloud, "Hot damn Vietnam," part sign of his cheer and part signal to his daughter that if she thought her mother insane she could afford to batten down for more high water. She could come away from that keyhole and sit at the dining-room table and hear some truly odd music from *him.*

A Local Boy

The Milledgeville Mole bears down upon himself with ruby-red precision. He takes coffee in his tea. His underwear is stained. There are global coordinates in his brain. The activation quotient for the bank robbery is below the level at which he would need find a gun and commence. The doughnuts are more important, from Ryall's, where the heavy girl in the weird old-fashioned light-green uniform dress is smart and nice to him. Her teeth are okay, and his are not.

His camp on the riverbank across from where Sherman camped is a dismal mess. Coons came and redid the feng shui the last three nights running. He feels there is mildew and coon spit on all his effects, even on the Grundig console radio that weighs a hundred pounds that he cannot move or listen to because there is no power but which looks very good there, like he is somebody. With all the coon spit and the mildew he would most like a flood and then a fire, or a fire and then a flood, to clean away the soot, or maybe it would be better to move altogether. Where did Sherman camp next, he wonders. Go with the flow, historically thinking. Why did Sherman not become President? Why Grant? Why is he, the Milledgeville Mole, an unemployed lout and not a fine bank president with a Rotary Club meeting this morning—a breakfast with a steam table!—or the owner say of the big Ford dealership out 441? He would live in a big house out on the lake and his pets would be dogs, big expensive dogs you take to the vet in their own SUV. He would not be predated upon by coons. The coons took every generic fig newton he had. A coon, he has noticed, does not leave something for later and a coon does not overlook anything, ever. They are like smell itself, if that makes sense. They should be used in airport security.

He flew to Las Vegas for the purposes of playing in the World Series of Poker and to play guitar with the group Van Halen but neither of these ventures worked out. He *fell back on*—he was a little tired of the expression to fall back on, but it was handy, and his mother had used it a lot in instructing him on how to live—he fell back on house painting for two weeks after that. The Las Vegas thing did not work out at the Milledgeville airport, where he had no identification to get on the plane with. A plane is not a Greyhound bus, he is fond of saying, or was, he no longer is. God his shoes are thin and rank and shitty-looking. If he could steal a pair of stout shiny shoes it would be a way of feeling better about things. He wonders where he is in the water column of history. He feels he is sideways to a lamb and talking to the worms. A school girl kicked him with a pair of these shoes they wear that have contrasting stitching like big dental floss, and he would like a pair of those, very effective weird-looking shoes. "Excuse me," he periodically says to himself, "I have to go kill someone now."

Mao

When we see the baby, it is swaddled in a tight charcoal wool coat that suggests Chairman Mao. It is held gently in place beneath the seat of a buckboard by the hobnailed boots of the coachman. From the baby's vantage the seat above it is a maneuver of wood and steel, and the boots of the coachman are towers of oiled leather. The heel of each boot holds a fold of the Mao coat to the buckboard floor. The jarring and jolting of the buckboard produces a finally pleasant aggregation of shocks that affect the child with the sopor of morphine. It is a not unhappy baby.

When the baby is older, and all of these impressions that can be are assimilated—when all of the available archival film is properly on sprocket and in register—the arrangement of the seat over the baby will come to suggest the underside of a flowerbox of the window variety. The springs on which the seat is supported will suggest in his memory ice tongs. This conceit is enriched and a bit confusing for there are actual ice tongs in the buckboard proper, and the baby will soon enough see them. There is ice in the buckboard. The coachman is the ice man, or would be, but that he is the ice woman. The baby's perspective up the towers of oiled leather does not at first permit it to know that it is the ice woman.

When the ice woman judges that the baby is large enough to ride on the seat without falling off, she puts it there, propped in a corner and held periodically by her hand. From the seat proper the baby can see the ice and the tongs and the ice woman delivering the ice. The tongs look angry and weird, but because he has seen the similar springs under the seat, holding the two of them up, the baby thinks of them as friendly things. He will come in time to see the tongs as not unlike the jaws of giant ants. But for now he is but a bouncing baby boy looking like a small bag of potatoes in a tight woolen bag on a buckboard seat. He has a small red hat.

His pursed red lips, like a cherry in the flat expanse of his potato face, make the ice woman want to eat him up. She does indeed kiss him with a wild unmotherly hunger that makes cannibalism tenable as she does it. She forces herself not to eat him up. He is grateful without knowing it, and likes her very much, knowing it. He comes to be her baby. Whose baby he really is, who she really is—in short, all of the film we do not have in archive- we do not know and we do not care.

We would like to instruct you not to care either. If you are the sort who must care, and must know things, we would politely suggest that this entertainment, if that is what it is, is not for you. The baby is not for you, nor hobnailed boots holding it down safely to the jarring wagon floor, nor the baby potatoed up into the hard corner of the seat in the freezing air about the ice wagon, its frozen lips a happy juicy red that the woman kisses with unmotherly abandon because she is not the mother, perhaps, or perhaps she is, or perhaps mother or not she just can't resist kissing the red lips given that all she has in her life is cometh-ing with other people's ice the livelong clodhopping day, watching her horse's road apples fall into the road and steam there and be rolled into by the wagon wheels—none of this is for you, and we give you your money back, no need for the door to necessarily hit you in the back on your way out, Jesus Christ Almighty. You will misinterpret, if you were to stay, seeing the woman dismount the wagon periodically and go behind a tree and virtually outright *neck* with the baby she gets so hungry for him. This affection is relieved with plenty of proper nuzzling, and it all tickles and delights the baby, who is for it the happiest baby alive and who ever was alive, but you won't be around to observe that. No, you will have bolted on behalf of the baby, to report crimes against humanity, and to watch an important show on TV. We know that one of your insurance policies is about to expire, and we are not going to tell you which one until it is too late. You have chapped our ass, and the baby's ass, and the ice woman's ass, entire. Get out. Your entire existence is predicated on chapping ass. You exist only to mint the dull coin of your bourgeois outrage, and to hand out this coin to the disinterested bystander, whom you presume to be the population of the whole world (now that you have "pluralized" it and "globalized" it). You are some kind of beggar in reverse, a beggar handing out moral alm no one asked you for. Let us tell you something: you can get away with that shit down here, but if we find this begging going on in Heaven or Hell, either one, there is going to be real and final trouble for you. We will stuff that coin and all the public-opinion syrup that lubricates it up both your ends. You will come to realize what nice guys we were to let you cant on down here and sing your jingles and dance your outrage jigs so happily.

Leave us and the baby Mao and the ice woman alone.

Yeltsin Dancing

To Putin I have given over everything but the nuclear suitcase. As dense as it is, I feel pretty light on my feet with only the suitcase on my hands. I look good with it, my white hair and the red suitcase. It got stuck under the bed and I popped a latch off extracting it, regrettable but the other latch holds. The landlady was demanding the rent and I had to move quickly.

Moreover, I have found the nuclear suitcase to be a superior chick magnet. Westerners in the know assure me that it can hold its own, a nuclear suitcase, with a BMW. I have replaced the cyanide vial in the handle with a 3-pack of condoms. I consider this a practical post-Cold-War accommodation and not a sacrifice to the original genius of the design. I am more likely to contract an STD than I am to have to deploy the suitcase.

I have learned to dance and believe it to be good for my heart. I do not subscribe to the platform of cardiovascular benefits said to accrue from exercise, I take simple and uplifting joy, the heart's first and final food, from the radiance of the disco ball. In attempting to sing along with some Bee Gees cuts I have come to appreciate their talent. They are, in their lyrics, pure exotica to the Eastern mind, rather the aural equivalent of Levis. They can reach higher registers than even Michael Jackson as a child did, I believe.

Putin is fucking up, or not, I pay it no mind. He is a strong man, so if he is fucking up, it is strong fucking up.

Yes, Putin is a strong man, but the delicacy of his fingers worries me. My own are thick pink wretched protuberances, manly. His are . . . his are lady fingers, which disturb me, which disturb everyone, if I may presume, on a man. But let us not dwell on the matter of Putin's adolescent-snake fingers and my fat pan-sausage fingers. After all, I have the suitcase.

The suitcase I gave to Putin, and familiarized his creepy fingers with the lethal toggles and keyholes and buttons thereof, is a dummy. This fact he will never discover. Even if he is moved to deploy his suitcase, which he will not be, any more than was I, he will attribute the ensuing non-end of the world to mechanical dysfunction of the suitcase, not to fraudulence of the suitcase. He will shake his head at the irony of the faulty nuclear suitcase—no better than any other modern technical manufacture, the portable red seat and soul of universal destruction!—and call for a red phone and be on about the business of ending the world. The false suitcase will never be exposed as such. It will sit innocent in the fallout, forgotten.

I have an opportunity to procure some dance instruction from one or another of Travolta's instructors for one or another of the movies, I am uncertain as to which. When I dance, sometimes I have an odd vision of myself as the American comedian Jack Benny. Then, standing beside me, but not dancing, is his manservant,

Rochester, on his face the kindest smile of disapproval. I should not be, the smile seems to say, boogying. I *know* I should not be boogying, I want to say, who are you, Rochester, to presume—when, of course, I see that Rochester is not really there and I, having lost the beat, am bumbling in the sparkling light on the dazzling plastic floor. I check my bearings and locate my real nuclear suitcase under my table and my drink on my table. In the old days the parasol in my drink was a radio but these days the parasol is not a radio.

I am free now, too, to have a dog. I did not think it fair before to subject a dog to presidential protocols. And my dear Naina objected. Now we have parted, she and I, and I leave any explanation of that to her. I wish her well. I consider a dog.

None of the girls drawn to me, with or without the power of the suitcase, has voiced an objection to my having a dog. For this and other reasons, like their modern underwear, I am fond of their company. The difficulty with having a dog, from the perspective of a free dancing man who can destroy the world, resides merely in selecting which breed. After that the matter is downhill. I know how to look at a pedigree and I know how to evaluate a puppy. If you have been leader of the second-most powerful nation on earth, the elected leader, and the first such to leave office voluntarily, you know how to administer the puppy test. You place him on his back and hold him there with the palm of your hand and see if he accepts it and stays, or struggles to free himself.

Many of the girls who have come to me have been in the movies as James Bond girls. They are relieved to discover that the suitcase is real, unlike Bond's gadgets, which they with some measure of disgust dismiss as phony, all. I wonder at their naivete—what did they expect?—but with girls of this sort, looking the way they do, silicone bombshells, I would be a bit naive myself to point out the lunacy of thinking James Bond should be possessed of real weapons. It occurs to me that Putin is like James Bond in this regard, a humorous conceit.

I have given some thought, as I dance and have many perfect girls and visit kennels, that I might seek employment. What I would most like to be is a television weatherman. I detect that one has little need for a background in meteorology, as indeed the news broadcasters are not required to be, or to have been, reporters. I have this fuzzy vision: dancing in place, my dog at my side and my suitcase in my hand, I point at snow on the map, my white hair looking like snow itself over my florid face, a bursting red tomato of happiness, applause issuing from the studio audience of Bond girls. I call my show "The Good News of Bad Weather." The suitcase is in view at all times as I predict dire weather. What fine irony! Even the girls appreciate it: the bad weather is in the red thing at my side, they know. I am *so* not James Bond, they say. This is true.

With or without such a sinecure, do I not have the world by its *yaitsi*? Few men evolve to such Elysian fields in their lifetime. I am lucky, lucky man.

Yeltsin Spotted Abroad in a Bar

We've got to get these wagons unloaded. The channel, tubing, I-beam, pipe, rod, conduit, connectors, the milled bombs, the forged doohickeys—I forget what they're called, are those *bells*? Why are we stocking bells?—those drilled blocks, the bolts, the cams, tailpipe, Torquemada, tensiometers, and if that is a case of Hi-Bounce Pinky I can't believe it, but maybe we are to improve our morale with ball games, unload them too, unload it all. The mattresses, the dressers, the mannequins, the raincoats, the marshmallows, the monster makeup, the marble cake, the crabs, the electrical tape, the torque wrenches, the pills, the mustard plasts, the canaries, the tomato starts, the non-medicine, the dogs, the magazines, the men's underwear, the dailies, the trusses, the small-caliber arms, the hex nuts, the candy. Did anyone see my wife drive up? Might have sat there a bit and then eased off? I have found her before down at the corner pottoed after easing off like that, no honking or attempt to notify me that she's here, just sits there two minutes looking straight ahead and then eases down to Raben's and has about six gin and tonics before anybody can get there, I have no idea what it is all about.

I have no idea what you and your wives are all about and I have never seen any of them at the loading dock or in Raben's I don't think—there is never anyone in there but my wife and a bartender who appears to be mute, and possibly deaf, who at first I thought was Boris Yeltsin and nothing yet has made a very strong argument that it is not Boris Yeltsin except that I don't know how he'd get here and get employed, etc. My wife's odd behavior is so . . . *odd* that I finally decided that if it *was* Boris Yeltsin maybe *that* was so odd that it began to explain her behavior, because nothing else did. She sits there and is truculent if that is the word, she kind of pouts, and says nothing, as I sort of console her off the stool and steer her out. Defiantly sad, is that better, yes, and she doesn't look at Yeltsin, but Yeltsin looks directly at us, intently, as if he has no American manners; I don't know for a fact that some Europeans have the manners of children when it comes to looking directly at what they find curious, but I think I have heard something to that effect, and if I have then this looking right at us of Yeltsin's is another circumstantial thread or tiny fact or twin premise upon which I base the conjecture that it is Boris Yeltsin actually tending bar in Raben's right here in Youngstown. There is no talking to my wife about it. If I say "Is that *Boris Yeltsin* serving you these drinks so fast?" she looks at me incredulously and does not say a word. If I say "Why do you not wait for me?" and "Why are you smashed?"— nothing. She goes to bed and sleeps well and there is no mention of any of this until the next time it happens.

None of you has had your wife do this? Have any of you been in Raben's and seen this Yeltsin character? Well, somebody go, I'm feeling a little isolated here.

Yeltsin and Canaries

I have procured a cage of canaries to go with the red nuclear suitcase, literally and aesthetically balancing me as I move from room to room in the free-market world. They look good together, in one hand the fluttering yellow birds inside the brass wire, the red anodized solid bomb valise in the other, white-haired I tottering stoutly between them, these my chief worldly possessions. The Porsche given me by Kohl I have lost. I have a toilet kit and a preserved leech in a bottle. I am fond of this in a way hard to understand. I do not know how I acquired it. The leech is beautifully segmented and looks like prime, chewy licorice in saline. The bottle cap is matching black. It is all in all a handsome if unusual accoutrement for a traveling dancing nuclear man.

Something somewhat alarming seems to be happening to, or with, or on, or in, or about—I hardly expect to get the English preposition right, whoever can—my fingers. They are shrinking and drying. More precisely, I sense that they are stubbifying and desiccating, becoming, that is, more blunt and more psioritic. They are becoming small fat white bratwursts as dry as toast. It will be difficult soon to carry the suitcase and the birdcage. I have the hope that if I can sling some blood into them that my fingers can grow, reverse this trend. You may see me on the dance floor whirling in an excessive-looking way, arms out like a child pretending to be a gyrocopter. I am aware that this is inelegant dancing, trust me, but I sacrifice style to health, or under health, or into health, whatever. I think most sympathetically of the cartoon character's three-fingered hand as I seem to tend that way myself. And small stubby hands do not attract chicks. I keep them hidden, or safely in prominent view when holding the red suitcase. No one regards *what* holds the suitcase. No one regards *who* holds the suitcase. The red suitcase diverts attention from the very disco ball itself.

Dancing is the meat-eater's meditation. When you have a disco ball overhead and a plexiglass floor of flashing neon underfoot and 120 decibels in your ear bones, you are nowhere else but in the room and thoughtless.

Working for Brother Catcard

Working for Brother Catcard has been fun. I got to see the whole iceberg incident, from the bow. The pastries are, I am told, and I do not have the wherewithal to doubt, as good as they are in France. My chi is in a super-flow state. I liken it to spoon-beaten magma.

Sister Willetail has improved morale with her good cheer and legs, but I am not pruriently concerned with her. The danger levels on the floor of operations are under control. If a worker gets hurt, he pretty much disappears entirely and there is not the issue of grisly remains.

We all got presents for Christmas, though it was stressed that the giving and the getting was not religiously affiliated, that the date was arbitrary more or less, at the top of the year, more a fiscal-holiday proposition. Once people started unwrapping their things they forgot to be aggrieved that we were calling it Christmas. I got a satellite-grade gyroscope. Benny and Lamar—whom I had not seen since 1960 when they were in the fourth grade, who rescued me from the mob when I was in the second grade in Ocoee Florida by schooling me at marbles, whose sister (Lamar's) was the first girl I took prurient interest in, though I did not know what prurient interest actually was yet—showed up.

They sat in plastic-webbed lawn chairs and opened their gifts, which appeared to be candy bars, but there had to be a little more to them (the candy bars) than that, because it is fair to say that Benny and Lamar sat there regarding these things mezzed out and beatific, if you can say beatific of grisled old bum-looking dudes nobody has ever seen before except me who saw them as fine-looking (if poor) children in 1960 in a schoolyard in the orange grove that was then Ocoee Florida. Ocoee Florida is now effectively Disney World and Benny and Lamar are, as I say, bums or bum-equivalents, and that they showed up and sat there in odd cheap non-company chairs no one else was sitting in and were mesmerized by candy-bar equivalents is just one of the reasons working for Brother Catcard has been so fun.

There is a preponderance of this equivalence thing; equivalents abound, to the extent that the whole experience at Brother Catcard's is kind of an equivalent itself, an equivalent to working, you might say. You might say the danger is an equivalent to danger, the injuries equivalent to injuries (hence no body parts). Christmas is an equivalent to Christmas, not Christmas. The presents are equivalents to presents. This can be seen in just the two I have so far listed: a gyroscope from a *satellite*? A candy bar that turns the bum unwrapping it into a stoned fool? Two bums that are supposed to be the same two children you briefly knew fifty years ago and have not seen since? And you have no doubt as to who they are, immediately? Is that not an agreeable equivalent to having lost your mind?

I can hear the sandhill cranes overhead. Bats are friendly. This is impossible to credit. Brother Catcard likes us all to be happy and friendly but it has not made us like bats, and that we are all happy and friendly is as hard to credit, or harder, than that bats are friendly. This is just one of my private calculations. I make private calculations the livelong day. You recall the song "I've been working on the railroad/all the livelong day"? Well, we sort of have that cheer here, working in the equivalent to working for Brother Catcard. Even when Floorchief Mayo yells at you it is an equivalent to yelling and is not to be carried heavily in the heart. If your sphericals are spherical and if your tubers grow through the correct holes in the little dirigible chassis, Floorchief Mayo's yelling does not mean shit to a tree, if I may try to quote Grace Slick, in whom I once did take prurient interest, but never met. What happened to Grace Slick? This is another zone of my private figuring on the factory floor.

What if her parents had named her Gorky Slick? I don't think I'd be quoting her, in that event, or I'd be quoting her as singing something else entirely, would be my inclination had she been Gorky and not Grace. Small forces have large resultants. This is one reason Floorchief Mayo gets worked up about the tiny holes and the tiny tubers. A microwave oven, in the same line of reasoning, would derange the guidance chips for the bomblets, and we must consequently heat our lunch things in conventional toaster ovens and on hotplates, which return to old-fashionedism I frankly heartily enjoy whether it is slow or not. You also have a high incidence of people burning the dook out of themselves in the break room but I have seen no real complaining.

Lamar and Benny were given positions on the line, which surprised me but should not have. It is possible that they had already been hired by the time they joined us at the Christmas party, or they were being watched in the interest of hiring them according to how they took the candy-bar equivalents, etc. Let me say a word or two about that. Big Brother is Watching You, which once was a somber and dire prophetic warning of some sort as far as I can tell, is now such a given that we are frankly a little amused at the alleged concern the notion is said to have once raised. *Of course* he is watching you, is our position: what else would he be doing? Who would watch us if he didn't? The idea that we might not be watched is altogether foreign, and frightening. We want to be watched.

I watched Benny and Lamar on the line. They were mercury rollers. That's where everyone with a fine hand starts, a little surprising because Benny, at least, appears to have the shakes, but I may be extrapolating from the condition of his nose, which looks whisky-rubricated. Oh, that is too poetic and probably inaccurate. It looks as red as an angry scrotum. By which I mean one that has been used and then not used when it would like to have been used. But Benny looks steady there with the mercury, and Lamar still has a bit of the fine cut he had when he was nine. His sister must have been ten, eleven, twelve when I noticed her legs. She was wearing short shorts and her legs were tight and long, and the shorts were tight on her legs, like say a rubber band on an eggplant. I know this is a stretch but this was decades ago and I was a child not yet ruined by thoughts of this sort and now I am an adult who is. I have license. And, as I say, if not that clearly, working here for Brother Catcard is really all about manifesting an equivalence to making sense. We manifest an equivalence to working and an equivalence to being adult.

It occurs to me watching Benny and Lamar roll the mercury through the chutes to the atomizers that they are still essentially playing marbles, which is exactly what they were doing when I first saw them fifty years ago. And they were very good marble players, which is how, and I suppose why, they could afford to take me under wing and school me. We spent the bulk of the school day in a large yard worn to smooth dirt and full of incipient gangsters kneeling down playing marbles all over it. They, Benny and Lamar, did not even flinch when I showed up with the cheap goofy marbles my father got for me because that was exactly what you wanted to put into games and lose when you were learning how to play. One day early on some other boys wanted to beat me up, because I was new or had shoes, I am not sure which, or both, and Benny and Lamar stopped it by a simple military positioning: Lamar stood up to the gang in front and Benny flanked the leader and just stood there, and the gang walked off. At some time later Lamar took me in the bathroom and unwrapped some adhesive tape on his big toe and showed me that it was nearly cut off, held on by a piece of skin, and then somewhere in there I went to their house and saw their huge box of marbles, a cardboard box the size of a TV beside the kitchen door. And I got on the bus behind Lamar's sister, which is when I saw the legs and the shorts from about a foot and a half in front of my face, going up and strong.

One of the natural developments to Big Brother's Watching You is that he keeps a file on us, and we are not discouraged from knowing what is in that file, in contradistinction, I think, to how it worked before when people felt that Big Brother's Watching You was prophetic and wrong. In that day, if I have it right, people did not know what Big Brother had on them in that file, and they were therefore correct to be worried and suspicious of being watched. But today we know. My file says, for example, "Mentally disturbed.

Hire him. He wants to make private calculations the livelong day. Let him." So I have no worries.

I suppose we are supposed to get worked up about this new development that Brother Catcard has had a dalliance with Sister Willetail, because it violates workplace ordinance, or ordinations, some ord-, or, if it doesn't violate rules, because we want to have had a dalliance with Sister Willetail ourselves, and that we haven't or can't and Bro Catcard has and can violates us and makes us jealous. But I am OK with the whole schpoo. Do I want her? Yes I do. May I have her? Probably not. Does this fact, like about five million equivalent facts in my life, distinguish the situation to the point I need to get worked up? No. Rules in the equivalent workplace are, after all, equivalents to rules in the workplace. Bro Catcard and Sister Willetail should prosecute their voyage as best they can. In Brother Catcard's file it will read "Wanted Sister Willetail. Got her."

Last night one of the metal buildings in the compound blew over, and this morning everyone is out in the rubble on the slab, kicking through the ruined stock and supplies and, strangely, giggling at this and that. Balls of yellow and pink insulation are blowing around like tumbleweeds. The big Zeiss crystal lens is unhurt and is to be picked up and carried to an intact building. Right now a forklift is being fitted with real sheepskin sleeves that will slip over the forks so that the glass is not scratched. The glass ball—that is basically all it is, except of course it is some rare fine German glass—weighs as much as a bull. This right here is one of the perversities of being here. This ball could be picked up by suction discs fitted to the arms of not even the largest robot we have made for the army, picked up and set down wherever you tell the robot to put it, and that could be in any impossible place up to

125 feet off the ground, or 125 feet under ground after it digs a hole with its other arm while holding the ball, and it can *throw* the ball a half mile—and yet Brother Catcard or someone above him deems that, after a tornado, for some reason, new technology must accede to old, and here comes sheepskin and a towmotor and an alcoholic driving the towmotor.

Benny is on the forklift. They haven't even sprayed the ball with the Kevlar beryllium foam, which they also have the capacity to do, so that virtually nothing, to include some missiles, can harm it. Here comes alcoholic-looking Benny wheezing and grinning on a towmotor with alcoholic-looking furry yellow forks out in front. He's got the forks about man-high and is making reckless speed across the rubble on the slab, jangling the forks even in their shearling booties, and as he gets near the ball he lowers the forks and slows to a good professional approach speed and it is easy to see that Benny is an old forklift man and that what he is doing is picking up a giant marble, and I stop cringing. I start marveling. I like to marvel, but I often do not. I marvel in this instance because I have known this man for fifty years, although I did not see him for the fifty years between second grade and now, and what I saw him do then and what I see him do now is concern himself with marbles. Is there a God? Has something or someone determined that Benny and marbles are a thing? There is a vending machine still standing in the ruins and I get a package of those small powdered doughnuts and eat them as Benny drives the Zeiss ball on the towmotor carefully out of sight. The sugar is cool on my fingers, strangely menthol.

We have received news that the Zeiss ball has been shipped over the high seas on a wooden sailing ship to Pondicerry India for use in an ashram temple there. A hole in the top of the temple will admit a shaft of strong light that will strike the ball and be refracted around the temple in a way that will calm the spirit. The effect of this light, Brother Catcard says he is told by telegram from India, as it will be uniquely refracted by our crystal ball, will be "ineffable." Insofar as the ball never did anything while it was here to calm the spirit, we are not aggrieved to learn of its better home, as it were. Brother Catcard also tells us that our time here is over, that the fallen building was a harbinger for the falling of our entire mission here. This too produces no outpouring of woe. It is the equivalent to failure, to being let go, to seeing one's way of life end as we know it, to the end of "family," and so forth, to perhaps not even being watched by Big Brother, to not having damning things in our files, to not even having files, and we are fine with the news, we are but equivalents to lost people. Equivalents to lost people, we discover, are not lost.

When she arrives, Lamar's sister, who should be sixty, is thirty-five years old and in very good shape. She looks like certain movie stars from the forties whose names I have never managed to match with their faces and whose faces all look, more or less, alike. The cheeks are high, the hair is swept back up and off the face, there is a good smile, red lipstick, bosom, good cheer. Lamar's sister is wearing the equivalent to those same cutoff jean shorts and a red-plaid yoked shirt with pearl snaps. We are instantly agreeable and without the difficulties that strain strangers, because we are only the equivalents of strangers. Equivalents to strangers are instantly intimate. I say this nonsense to her: "God, babe, I have been waiting for you a long time, it feels as if I was even holding my breath, I can breathe now, I didn't realize I was waiting for you—"

"Yes, shut up."

There is a powdered doughnut in its cellophane package on

the nightstand. Lamar's sister carefully extracts the doughnut and regards it in the light and takes a tentative lick. There is white powder on her red lips and she smiles and an air of menthol fills the room.

Utopia

A man in a cigar-colored suit is not to be trusted, and frankly my aversion to that one over there goes well beyond mistrust: I outright do not like the son of a bitch. A cigar-colored suit!

I am pursuing my dissertation on agiation. That is the new science of getting old. In case you need to know what I am talking about. You probably don't. Sometimes I myself wonder why anyone needs to know anything about agiation, when for thousands of years people just did it without being told a goddamn thing about it and they got along fine, getting old right on schedule and getting in their final pajamas, etc. I wonder why anyone needs to know anything about anything when you get right down to it. In this same spirit of wonderment I wonder why everyone has to suddenly be on the phone all the time. Everyone has suddenly decided they have to know what everyone else is up to at every minute of the day. How did this happen? We have all become The President.

There is a new society forming. It is going to allow only running water in a house, a three-channel TV, a rotary-dial phone, a wringer washing machine, and one car.

When the cigar-colored-suit-wearing asshole is not wearing that, he is wearing a sky-blue one! It would be fun and gratifying to see a car knock him out of his shoes. There they would sit, some kind of Italian superiority, empty on the road, nearby which groans the lump who wore them to that forlorn spot. The ambulance might be forever in coming. What will become of the shoes? I despise that asshole. I would hope that a bum would come along and fit himself into the shoes and shamble off in them, perhaps right by the paralyzed face of the owner, who could just force himself to groan, "Muuhshoooos!"

"Yeahnow," the bum says, "1 clickin' and clackin' down the track *now*."

No Empress Eyes

No Empress Eyes In Here had first been named No Empress, then No Empress Eyes, and then the owner's daughter, hearing the name but not knowing it applied to a horse, said, "No empress eyes *in here*," and the final name was set. She was ten years old, the daughter, and lived in New Jersey. They then told the daughter that the horse No Empress Eyes In Here disappeared during the Kentucky Derby when she fell through a trapdoor in the track. She went down a laundry chute not to China but to some other inscrutable place no one knew anything about or where it was, so "She might as well," the daughter said, "have gone to China," for all they could do about it. Thereafter the horse was known as No Empress Eyes Down There.

There was a boy in Kansas, also ten, who dreamed of inventing a new kind of combine that would not harm animals when it came upon them in the wheat. Specifically the boy was thinking about fawns, who were told by their mothers, who had galloped away, to stay put no matter what, and who, the fawns, would stay put no matter what, no matter if a combine with a 24-foot-wide worm blade came upon them and scooped them up and sprayed them into the wheat in pieces no larger than the wheat. This very much bothered the boy, who wanted to be a farmer badly except for this one thing, turning baby deer into bloody wheat. So he wanted a humane combine. He thought and thought and could not come up with an idea for a combine that would pick up the deer and set it to the side and pet it and send it trotting off to the place its mother had hightailed it to before abandoning it in the field with the diesel monster bearing down on it. He wanted the mother deer to be issued a citation for negligent parenting too, and maybe have the combine call the department of child welfare and take the fawn away from the mother as it did children from human parents who did things not nearly as bad as leave their children in the tall grass in front of huge machines. But he would never invent a machine that would do all this, that was fantasy thinking, he wanted a real machine to really rescue the fawns, forget about justice. He thought and thought and finally arrived at a compromise suggested by the man at the Brandt's meat market in Lucas: the fawn could be scooped up and blown whole into another chamber, probably dead, but not in a million pieces. Okay, the boy said, okay. Until he could invent the new combine he drove the conventional combine so slowly that everyone was unpleased with him during harvest but he did not care. He was through with scooping up fawns. He was disgusted with these people, like John Deere, who probably called themselves that for a joke, and a joke about killing deer was not funny. They had a slogan "Runs like a Deere" that ought to be "Like Running *Down* a Deere," he thought.

After the horse she'd named fell through the track and no one did anything about it, the horse owner's daughter felt she'd had it with these people and ran away. It went well for a while, was not too frightening when she was on the bus, but then she was walking a long way and in the country and she hid in a field, and a giant machine came up on her with a big steel like barber-pole thing turning and cutting the grass, and it stopped, the machine, coming at her, but the barber pole did not stop turning and hissing, and a boy got out of the glass cabin on top of the machine letting blaring music come out with him, like Queen, or Aerosmith, and she wondered what kind of hicks they had out here wherever she was. "Well," the boy said, "do you want to run like a deer or be run *down* like a deer?" That was about the coolest thing she had ever heard anyone say whether he was a hick or not, and she got in the cabin and they mowed some more field.

Then they went to his cave. It was in the side of a creek bank with no water in the creek and it was filled with a lot of appliances that did not work because there was no power. He had floor lamps in it with fringe on the shades, and a big kitchen stove, and an old TV with a wood cabinet that looked like an aquarium full of dull green algae and no fish, and a brass bed that was brown from the moisture in the cave. There were no bats. The boy said he wanted bats but none ever came in that he saw. There were only dried-up roots hanging from the ceiling. These felt like bats when you touched them. If it were her cave she would trim the ceiling, the horse owner's daughter thought.

They decided they had to tell someone where she was but the boy was afraid he would be arrested for kidnapping and molesting her. "All you did was run me down like a deer," the girl said, suddenly wondering what became of the jockey on her horse that had gone down the hole in the track. Really, nothing had been said at all about the jockey; it was a thoroughly unsatisfying business, that horse disappearing, and horse racing in general, and rich people, and poor people, the whole earth was messed up, and now here was a boy talking about molesting her who had not touched her, who had no idea what molesting even meant. She didn't either. "Why don't you molest me then?" she said.

"Good idea, since I will be arrested for it." The boy threw himself on the moldy bed. "I don't know what *molest* means, actually."

"I don't either. Whatever it is, don't do it."

"Okay. I won't." The boy had crossed his feet and put his hands behind his head. "*Man*," he said, "this is like *living!*"

They both envisioned living in the cave for a good long time away from horrible and boring horse racing and horrible and boring farming—"But farming is not boring, just horrible, and just the fawn grinding," the boy said—but they knew they couldn't make it very long in a cave. "That is *fan*tasy thinking," the boy said.

"No Empress Eyes Down Here," the girl said, and the boy did not ask what in the world was she talking about. He just got out of bed and adjusted his pliers on his belt and said, "Come on." He was very cool, in her judgment. They held hands crossing the field.

"I think holding hands is part of molesting," the girl said.

"Okay," the boy said. "I will be arrested." He clearly enjoyed saying *arrested*.

At the farm the boy's father called the Sheriff and reported having the girl with no more travail than he might have reported the wheat to be too wet to harvest, and his mother set a place at the table almost as if they had expected her and certainly as if she were a guest they were pleased to have and not a runaway with legal strings attached to her. If anyone was going to be arrested it was not going to be them, or even her, it seemed. The mother told her everything would be fine and she could plan to stay with them until they heard anything from the Sheriff.

"We want to live a long time together in the cave," the boy said.

"We'll have to run some Romex out there after dinner," the boy's father said, "in that case." He was eating and perhaps joking, perhaps not, you could not get a good look at his mouth for the food going in. He had on his belt the same kind of pliers the boy had on his. He wore jeans and non-pointy boots and no hat. These Kansas people were not like Texas people. The girl had had enough of Texas people with their ridiculous boots and jewelry, always around scaring the horses and trying to buy everything in sight. She had not seen a Kansas person try to buy anything and she had not heard one be loud. This was more like it. If they were going to run Romex to the cave, whatever that meant, she would help them.

The food was odd. "What's the name of this again?" she asked, about some balls of something like pancake they were eating in syrup. "Evilskeever," the woman said. "And this?" The girl took a bite of another food they'd served her to show she was not critical of it. It was also in a ball, but a mushy and not a cakey ball. "Ham and bean glob," the boy said. "It's the best." There was no salt and pepper in sight. Everything was served in a bland ball. These people had figured a few things out. At her house eating was a trial, a series of repellent exotic challenges, everything so seasoned that it stank. Out here you could relax and eat, it looked like, without worrying about it.

She had learned too that they had a horse—*one*, a working horse, named Carl. After this dinner of pancake balls and ham and bean mushballs they could put Romex on Carl and get her a little set of pliers for her own belt and head for the cave, and with her pliers she was going to tear off the roots coming out of the ceiling as her contribution to all the sense-making going on out here in the middle of nowhere. They could listen to Aerosmith or Queen or Genesis if they wanted to, they were doing things right out here. She hoped the Sheriff was corrupt or lazy or incompetent and did not call her father. Really, if a horse disappeared out here, there would be some answers for it, some answering for someone to do. A horse was not going to disappear out here. A horse named Carl did not disappear or do anything else ridiculous; he did his job and ate his feed and waited for his next job, which did not involve being skittish and violent and lame and sick and costing everyone so much money and anxiety that they got divorces and heart attacks. What they needed back in New Jersey was a horse named Carl and some ham and bean glob to settle their nerves. She was not going back if she could help it. "Man," she said suddenly, and everyone looked at her, "this is living!"

They laughed.

"I need some of those pliers."

"No problem," the father said, between gooey evilskeevers, of which he had eaten eighteen by her count. He was outright hoovering the evilskeevers. Another good sign.

Outside in the dusk in the farmyard the boy picked up a piece of baling wire and wound it loosely around her finger. He pulled out his pliers in a motion so quick that she wanted pliers all the more and he twisted the baling wire lightly until it snugged on her finger and then he clipped the twist close, leaving a loose ring of galvanized wire on her finger and them both appraising it. "You are my wife," the boy said. "Okay?"

"Sure," the girl said. "Sure." She fingered the sharp little nub of the clipped twist and made the ring travel around her finger. The father approached with a set of pliers and a small leather holster that looked old and oily and forgotten until now, and they put it on her belt.

They went fishing in their pond and the girl caught two catfish and the men caught nothing. With her own pliers the girl removed the hook from her catfish, the first fish she had ever caught. Seeing this, the boy said, "You have to bait your own hook too. If you don't, you will be arrested." At dark they went home. The kitchen was cleaned of all evidence of evilskeever and ham and bean glob, and the Sheriff had not called, and they went to bed. This was living.

About the Author

Padgett Powell is the author of six novels, including *The Interrogative Mood* and *Edisto*, which was a finalist for the National Book Award, and two collections of stories. His writing has appeared in *The New Yorker, Harper's,* and *The Paris Review*, as well as in *The Best American Short Stories* and *The Best American Sports Writing*. He has received a Whiting Award, the Rome Fellowship in Literature from the American Academy of Arts and Letters, and the James Tait Black Memorial Prize. Powell lives in Gainesville, Florida.